NEIL HUNTER

TO RIDE THE SAVAGE HILLS

Complete and Unabridged

LINFORD
Leicester

First published in Great Britain in 2016

First Linford Edition
published 2018

A catalogue record for this book is available
from the British Library.

ISBN 978–1–4448–3792–6

Published by
F. A. Thorpe (Publishing)
Anstey, Leicestershire

Set by Words & Graphics Ltd.
Anstey, Leicestershire
Printed and bound in Great Britain by
T. J. International Ltd., Padstow, Cornwall

This book is printed on acid-free paper

TO RIDE THE SAVAGE HILLS

Arizona, 1888: Marshal Ed Pruitt had been bringing Sam Trask to justice when, following an accident, Trask murdered the driver and escaped. Now Pruitt wants Bodie to bring Trask in before the wanted man can cross the line into Canada. But what should be a straightforward pursuit soon turns into something far more puzzling. Trask is a killer, yet people are willing to cover for him. As he rides the savage hills, facing bullets and treacherous weather, Bodie proves that he's the toughest manhunter the West will ever see . . .

Until 1889, the territory encompassing what would become Montana and North Dakota was known as the Dakotas, a large expanse of land with little organised law. Wild and open, it was policed by the hard-pressed office of the US Marshals, dedicated men who were responsible for enforcing the law over an uncompromising tract of land. Bringing law and order to the Dakotas was not easy. The marshals were few, the problems many, and they had an unenviable task that they undertook with the dedication that became their legend . . .

The formation of the states was recognised as unifying the former territory and opening a new era — yet in the time leading up to it, the Dakotas forged their own destiny, and the US Marshal service did its part — though, unofficially, not without a little assistance . . .

1

DAKOTA TERRITORY — 1888

Bodie opened his eyes and felt the harsh glare of the high sun on his face.

He made no attempt to move, because if he did, he knew it would hurt even more. He felt pretty sure his entire body was one solid bruise. If it wasn't, it should have been. He had been worked over on other occasions, so he knew what it felt like.

He closed his eyes again and shut out the bright light. He figured he might as well stay where he was until the pain eased off — but the way he was feeling, that might not be for a long time. He could taste blood in his mouth from a cut on the inside of his cheek and explored with his tongue to see if any teeth had been loosened. No; they felt secure. He became aware of a sharp pain over his left eye, and touching the spot, he felt the ragged gash that was still bleeding. He let his fingers trace the contours of his face. More than one cut. Bruised and already swelling. Lips split and bloody.

That would have been Cabot.

He recalled the way the big man had worked his fists inside the rawhide gloves he wore. It had been Will Cabot who had been so eager to hit out. The man had been coiled, ready to strike. And he had already shown his dislike for Bodie; so when the moment came he was the first to step forward, determined to prove himself. Maybe too determined.

Cabot was there to defend his friend. That was the pure problem. Cabot was defending his friend, Sam Trask. And Trask was the man Bodie was tracking — a wanted man on the dodge. He had been posted for the savage rape and murder of a woman. He had been on his way to jail when the coach taking him there had hit a section of broken trail and overturned.

There had only been two passengers in the coach: Sam Trask, in manacles, and Marshal Ed Pruitt, his escort. On the box was the driver, Clem Bogard. The coach had been hired to take Pruitt and his prisoner to Yankton, where he would await trial. The unexpected accident had resulted in Pruitt being injured; and while the lawman had been unconscious, Trask had found the key to his manacles in the marshal's pocket. He had freed himself and taken Pruitt's handgun.

When Pruitt had recovered enough to drag himself from the coach, he had found Clem Bogard dead from a bullet wound through the back of his head. If anything proved the point about Sam Trask, the cold-blooded murder of Clem Bogard was it.

★　★　★

Bodie had learned this background when he had spoken to Marshal Ed

Pruitt in Yankton. He had made a rendezvous with the marshal, following a summons from him. Bodie had known Pruitt for a number of years, and receiving a call from the man had aroused his curiosity.

Pruitt had come directly to the point, which was not unusual for him. The marshal was an experienced star packer, a man who had known his share of miscreants over the years. Good, bad, and downright miserable, he had seen them all.

'Now I ain't one for bad-mouthing a man,' Pruitt said, 'but what can I say about what Trask did? The stories are he's a mean sonofabitch. What he did to Clem — well it just tells all. Am I talking crazy, Bodie, or what? Maybe that bang on my head kind of left me addled, but what reason could he have had for that?'

Bodie was sitting across from Pruitt in the marshal's office, nursing a cup of coffee. He would have made the trip to see Pruitt for the coffee alone. 'How's the head, by the way?'

Pruitt still wore a bandage over the wound. 'Grateful I have a hard one,' he said.

He picked up a flyer from the desk and handed it to Bodie. It gave a description of Sam Trask, had a neat sketch of the man, and advertised the fact that there was a reward for him.

'I can tell you, Bodie, that's a damn good likeness of the man. Better than any photograph.'

Bodie read the flyer again — Wanted Dead or Alive. 'So why bring me in on this, Ed?'

'Tracks from the coach were headed due north, up towards the high country. Pretty lonely up there. And him on foot with no real supplies 'cept what he took from the coach, just the clothes he was wearing and a horse with no saddle. But he did take a rifle and a handgun. My gun.'

That had left a question in Bodie's mind. Where was Trask heading? He answered his own question when a map of the area pinned to the office wall drew his eye. Canada. Across the border lay Saskatchewan and Manitoba, where a man might easily lose himself — big, wide-open country, sparsely inhabited, and where US law would be out of its jurisdiction. It was as good a place as any for a wanted man to ride.

'Now I could go through all the motions and ask the Canadians for help,' Pruitt said, 'but dammit, Bodie, by the time I got all that signed and sealed, Trask could be up in the Yukon.'

Pruitt knew the border wouldn't stop Bodie. He would track his quarry wherever he chose to go. Which was why Ed Pruitt had brought the manhunter to Yankton.

'No paperwork. No tin star, Bodie. Just you trailing Trask and bringing him back. Hell, man, it's what you do best.'

Bodie stood and examined the wall map. From the point where Trask had walked away from the coach, the terrain was wild and empty. There were a hundred places a man could lose himself. Pruitt had pointed out the remoteness of the area. His idea about Canada fit the picture too. There was little between Trask and the border; nothing to prevent him disappearing into the great expanse of the country and vanishing.

'Bodie?'

The manhunter emptied his cup and crossed to refill it. Pruitt was watching him closely, awaiting his decision.

'I get supplies provided by your office?'

Pruitt gave a stifled laugh. 'You drive a hard bargain, Bodie.'

'Man has to make a living.'

* * *

A living? Getting beaten down by a bunch of mustangers. If that's the case, Bodie thought, *I need to change my priorities.*

He made the decision to stop debating matters and get to his feet. It was an easier-said-than-done proposition. It hurt. It hurt a lot; but Bodie was, if nothing else, a stubborn individual. Moving caused ripples of pain that felt as if they started at his feet and ran though him all the way to the top of his head. It wasn't the first time he'd been on the receiving end of a sound beating, but never one as thorough. He made himself a promise that somewhere along the line, Will Cabot would be repaid for what he'd done. Bodie admitted his thinking was petty, even childish, but he also decided the hell with that. He was in a petty and childish frame of mind right now, and the thought of the satisfaction to be gained from giving Cabot a taste of what he was suffering right now gave Bodie a warm feeling.

Eventually he stood upright — not as straight and tall as usual, but was on his feet. He remained there until the world stopped spinning, forced the sickness from his stomach and took long, deep breaths. Even that hurt. Bodie closed his arms around his body, pressing against his aching ribs, and convinced himself there were no breaks. His battered body still hurt, but at least he was standing again.

He took a long look around and recognized where he was. Yards away his horse stood, still tethered to a low tree branch. Bodie glanced down at his right hip. His Colt was still in his holster, held secure by the hammer loop. They had left him his weapons. He checked his horse again and saw the stock of his rifle jutting from the saddle-boot.

Bodie had tracked Trask up country, spotting where his trail led to the mustanger camp. He had even seen the horse from the coach in the corral, its company brand showing on its hip. When he had asked the question, the mustanger boss, Will Cabot, had turned on him and, backed by his crew, had set on him with a vengeance. The physical and verbal warning had been the same. Stay away from Sam Trask. Leave him alone.

So Cabot had initiated the beating, leaving Bodie bruised and bloody, but had let him keep his weapons. That left questions to be answered, but at that moment in time Bodie neither had the urge nor the ability to go into it. That would come later. The only concern in his mind was the fact Sam Trask had passed through the area. It was why Bodie was here. He had come looking for Trask, and one way or another he would find the man and haul him back to Yankton.

First he needed to get himself doctored. It wasn't going to do him any good chasing all over creation if he required tending. As reckless as he might be on occasion, Bodie had sense enough to know when he needed the services of a doctor.

2

When Bodie reached the town of Colton, he stabled his horse at the livery, asked where the town's doctor resided, and made the slow walk to the office.

Doc Meerschaum was in his early sixties, a round-shouldered and broad-faced individual with a fierce expression and a personality to match. Pale eyes viewed the world from behind steel-rimmed spectacles. He wore heavy mutton-chop whiskers as gray as his thick head of hair. He stared at Bodie silently pursing his lips as he examined the cuts and bruises on his face, and then told him to remove his shirt.

'I do not recognize you from the town,' he observed, his words revealing his German accent. 'Are you new here?'

'Yeah. And up to now I'm not impressed by the hospitality.'

For whatever reason, Bodie's remark amused the medical man. He gave a raspy chuckle. 'I never seem to be amazed at the propensity you Americans have for inflicting violence on each other.

'Just one of the things that makes us such a likable bunch.'

Meerschaum made soft tutting sounds as he viewed the livid bruises over Bodie's ribs. His powerful square hands were surprisingly gentle as he made his examination. He murmured to himself in his native tongue, carefully probing, and after a couple of minutes he nodded to himself.

'The good news is there are no broken bones. Your ribs are badly bruised, but no breaks. The bruises on your face also will heal in time, and the cuts. You are a lucky man, Herr Bodie.'

'Doc, we have different views on what being lucky means.'

'Ja. I meant you are lucky no broken bones have penetrated any organs. You will be extremely sore for a few days, but I can see you are a healthy and strong man. Tell me, do you heal quickly?'

'In my business I don't get much time to sit around taking it easy.'

'And out of interest, what is your business?'

'I look for men who have broken the law.'

'So a lawman?'

'Not officially . . . '

Meerschaum peered over his spectacles, working out what Bodie meant. He held up a finger. 'A bounty hunter.'

'Doc, I hope that isn't disapproval.'

'Herr Bodie, you are the first bounty hunter I have ever met.'

'Hell, you're the first German doctor I've ever met.'

Meerschaum's laugh was genuine. 'Then it is a special day for us both. Can you tell me who you are looking for?

'Feller called Sam Trask.'

'Not a name I'm familiar with.' Meerschaum brought a bottle of liniment and applied it generously to the bruises. 'This may sting a little, but it will help to ease the bruises.'

Bodie felt the liniment's warm flush increase until it became uncomfortably hot. 'Doc, what's in that damn stuff?'

'Only good things to help you heal.' Meerschaum produced a roll of bandages and proceeded to bind them tightly around Bodie's torso. 'This will need to stay in place for a few days. You should not do anything that will put a strain on those ribs.'

Bodie kept silent on that. Sitting quietly in a rocking chair was not on his list. Sooner or later he was going to have to get back in the saddle and pick up on Sam Trask's trail, sore ribs or not. Allowing too much time to slip by would only give Trask more time to get out of the area. Bodie was already losing out. He didn't intend to let that go on.

As he paid Meerschaum what he owed, Bodie asked, 'Doc, a couple of things. There a lawman in town? And

16

where would I get a good meal?'

'The marshal has an office back down the street. Turn right when you leave and you cannot miss it. For food there is Monty's Restaurant across the street there, just across from the jail. Monty is a good cook and the food is wonderful.'

'Grateful for that.' Bodie pulled on his shirt, taking his time because every move caused problems. He picked up his hat. 'I know where to find you.'

'When I hear you say things like that, I worry you are not about to do what I suggested.'

'I'm not about to go looking for trouble.'

'Something warns me you are a man who attracts it. Das ist so, ja?'

★ ★ ★

The marshal's office was located next to a general store on one side and a gunshop on the other. There was an alley between the law office and the gunshop, but not between the office and the store. They butted up together. Bodie was to find out the store owner, Ezra Pointer, was also Colton's part-time lawman.

The marshal's office was closed up. Bodie was still at the door when a solid-looking man wearing an apron over his clothes stepped out of the store. In his forties, he had thinning dark hair and keen eyes. He wore a thick neatly trimmed mustache on his upper lip. He held a broom in one hand and paused when he saw Bodie.

'Might not look like it, but I'm Marshal Pointer. Part-time. Rest I'm Ezra Pointer, store owner.'

'Nice to know there's only a need for a part-time lawman. Suggests Colton is a peaceful town.'

Pointer smiled. 'The other way to look at it is we're close to being a pretty dull town.' He reached out a long hand. His grip was firm. Bodie took it.

'Name's Bodie. I was directed here by the doctor.'

'Oh? I can infer from your face that you've been hurt?'

Bodie related his run-in with Cabot and his crew. A look of concern showed on Pointer's face.

'Not that I'm surprised. That outfit tends to cause trouble come rain or shine, and Will Cabot is the worst of them all.' He indicated the marks on Bodie's face. 'They because of Cabot?'

'And a set of bruised ribs the doc strapped up.'

'You here to swear out a complaint?'

'No. I just wanted to ask if you knew the man I'm trailing. Name of Sam Trask.'

Pointer's shifting eyes told Bodie he knew the name.

'Will you give me a minute? We can go in the office.'

Pointer turned and went back inside the store. He emerged, minus the broom and apron, shrugging into a dark jacket and brushing self-consciously at the badge pinned to his striped shirt. Back outside he led the short way to the jail, producing a key and unlocking the timber door. Bodie followed him inside. He noticed in passing that the windows on either side of the door had strong iron grilles over them.

It being a warm day, the inside of the office was close and dry. Pointer left the door open. Their footsteps echoed on the plank floor. It was a lawman's office just like a dozen Bodie had seen before. There was a gun rack holding a number of rifles and a brace of shotguns — Greeners, Bodie saw, securely chained in place; a wooden file cabinet, and wanted posters on the whitewashed walls. A door was at the rear, made from iron bars that would likely allow entry to the cell area. The place had the look of being well maintained.

'Take a seat, sir,' Pointer said, gesturing towards a ladder-back chair placed in front of the surprisingly large desk. Bodie eased himself down carefully and settled himself as Pointer took the swivel chair behind the desk. 'You look to be in some discomfort.'

'Cabot and his boys were in a mind to cause me some,' Bodie said.

Pointer stared at some point over Bodie's shoulder, and it was obvious he was considering his next words with care. It took Bodie less than a few heartbeats to figure out what the lawman was thinking.

'Marshal Pointer, we might as well get this said straight off. I'm not a lawman; I guess you have that worked out. To put it straight, I'm a bounty man. I chase after men wanted by the regular law and collect the rewards on them. Might not be to the delicate tastes of some folk, but until the law is strong enough to deal with things better, well . . . '

Pointer sank back in his seat, relief crossing his pleasant face. He laid his hands flat on the desk. 'Seems to me you covered everything I was thinking. And truth be told, a man wearing a badge can end up doing what you do. He chases criminals too. Gets paid as well, I suppose.'

'I've never actually thought on that. It's pretty close to the truth. But not everyone sees a bounty man in a clear light.'

They both turned as a shadow fell across the door. A smiling and attractive woman, around Pointer's age, wearing a dark gray dress, stepped inside. She was carrying a wooden tray that held a steaming coffee pot and a pair of china mugs. She placed the tray on the desk, then stepped back, nodding at Bodie.

Pointer said, 'This is Mister Bodie. He had a run-in with Will Cabot and his crew.'

'I'm sorry to hear that, Mister Bodie. Truth is, those mustangers can be an undisciplined bunch.'

'Yes, ma'am. I found that out.'

'I'll leave you to your official business, Ezra.'

Bodie half rose. 'Ma'am, thanks for the coffee.'

'You're very welcome,' she said, and left the office.

Pointer poured coffee for them both.

'When I mentioned Sam Trask, Sheriff, I saw you react.'

The lawman slid open a drawer, and after a little shuffling of paper he drew out a wanted flyer and held it up. It was the identical one Bodie had folded in his shirt pocket.

'That's all I have. To my knowledge, that man has never shown his face in Colton. Tell me, Mister Bodie, how did you learn about him?'

'Marshal from Yankton, Ed Pruitt, was escorting Trask for trial. Their coach was in a crash. Pruitt took a crack to the skull. While he was unconscious Trask freed himself, took the marshal's gun and escaped on one of the coach horses. But he also shot and killed the coach driver before he left.'

'Poster says he stands accused of murder and rape. He kills one man but leaves the other. Conflicting behavior.'

'Makes you think, Marshal.'

Pointer sipped from his mug. 'How do you figure it?'

'Not for me to judge. Ed Pruitt asked me to go after Trask. I'll do that and hand him over. Marshal's office is stretched pretty thin these days, and if Trask decides to jump over the border . . .'

'Into Canada?'

'Officially, Pruitt's department has no jurisdiction. He'd have to get permission from the local Canadian authorities. He might well get it, but you can be sure it would take a long time with things going back and forth. Trask could be so far away by then it might be a lost cause.'

'But you don't need permission, I take it?'

Bodie reached out to top up his mug. 'Your missus makes good coffee, Marshal Pointer.'

Pointer understood there was no more to say on the matter.

'The doc said Monty's Restaurant was a good place to eat.'

'It is. That what's next?'

Bodie nodded. 'Then a place to bed

down for the night. Let Doc Meer-schaum's liniment do its job.'

'His famous potion for all ills?' Pointer smiled. 'Truth is, it works. I had a badly sprained wrist a few months back. He treated it, and damned if it wasn't right as rain in a few days.'

'Food first, then a room.'

'Other end of town. The boarding house. I'll take a walk there while you eat. Ask Mrs. Toliver to have something ready for you.'

'Marshal, this town is making things easy for me.'

'I dare say once you ride on after Trask, things might not be.'

3

Sometime earlier Claude Tessler rode back into camp, tending his horse before crossing to confront Will Cabot. The look on his face drew Cabot's attention, and he waited until Tessler helped himself to coffee from the blackened pot set over the campfire.

'What in hell twisted your tail?' Cabot asked, sensing Tessler's mood.

'You want to know?'

Cabot sneered, his hard features twisting. 'Jesus, Claude . . . '

'He's in town,' Tessler said, gulping at the coffee. 'That manhunter. Bodie. I saw him big as life going into Doc Meerschaum's office. Looked like he was walkin' careful, like he was still hurtin''.

'You sure it was him?'

'Hard to miss, him bein' a big hombre, and with bruises showing where we beat up on him. It was him, Will. I done watched him walk down the street.'

Cabot took the makings from his shirt pocket and rolled himself a thin quirly. He fired up a match on his gun-butt, drawing deep of the smoke. He took his time looking around the untidy sprawl of the mustang camp, his mind working as he considered his next move.

'Get back to town,' he said. 'See if you can figure what that feller is up to. It's plain to see he didn't heed our warning. Do it quiet-like, but nose around. I need to find out if he's been talking to Pointer.'

'I could maybe crowd the lawdog a little, see what's going on.'

'Use your head, Claude. Ain't going to be smart riding the law. Pointer's no big-time lawman, but in Colton he packs a star. Just bide your time and walk soft around him. Go buy some supplies. Make it look like a genuine call to town. But stay easy.'

Tessler finished his coffee and tossed the dregs away. He made his way across to where their horses were tethered in a bunch and picked out one of the mules they used for carrying gear.

Watching him go, Cabot finished his smoke before he called out to his waiting crew. They sauntered across to pick up their own mounts and trailed out of camp, heading up into the hills where they would pick up the trail of the wild horse herd. They already had a dozen mustangs in a box canyon where one of the crew watched over them. Cabot had decided they needed another dozen or so before they herded them down out of the hills and made the trek to make trade with the stock. They would sell them off, as they had done before. The army was always on the lookout for fresh mounts, and Cabot also had a good contact for civilian trading. Ranches were good customers. Buying off Cabot saved them the bother of having to go out and chase the wild herds themselves, and for additional cash Cabot could offer his own men to break in the animals. It was a hard life and took hard men to put up with it. It suited Cabot. His crew was the same. They endured the hard, risky life because it allowed them the freedom of being men beholden to no one, and the rewards were well worth the effort.

As they trailed out of camp, leaving behind the cook and his helper and a couple of men to watch the remuda, Cabot found himself still concerned over Bodie. Having the manhunter around was something he could have done without. He hadn't said anything out loud, keeping the knowledge to himself, but he had heard about the man.

As a bounty hunter, Bodie had few equals. His reputation went ahead of him. He was a hard-driven man, never one to step back from any situation, and he was known to stay on a fugitive's trail until it was over. A man could run, but never — it was claimed

— far enough once Bodie was dogging his tracks.

'Son of a bitch,' Cabot murmured to himself.

As if he didn't have enough to handle without Trask showing up. He could have gone in a dozen different directions instead of seeking out Cabot. But that was the trouble with family; they tended to seek each other out when things went wrong. Cabot had no say in the matter now. He was bound to do what he could to help Sam Trask. After all, he was Cabot's son. Estranged maybe, and always in trouble. But he was Cabot's flesh and blood, and that had to count for something.

He suddenly found himself with a thin smile on his face.

'What in hell's making you so happy?'

The question came from one of his crew, a lanky thin-faced man called Jefferson. He had eased his chestnut mare alongside Cabot, and the question had formed when he saw his boss's expression.

'Why not?' Cabot said. 'Nice day, and everything's going my way.'

'If you say so, boss,' Jefferson said. 'Still don't make this dust taste any better, though.'

Jefferson frowned at the response. It wasn't like Cabot to say such things. He lost the thought then when he heard a yell from one of the crew. They were nearing the canyon and Jefferson was needed. He reined his horse aside and spurred it to catch up, his curiosity forgotten.

Cabot watched him go. He allowed he had been letting his attention wander. Trask's unexpected intrusion back into his life had been distracting him. Now was not the time for things like that. He needed to stay focused. If he wasn't careful, he might let himself blunder into a situation that could prove difficult to get out of.

* * *

Claude Tessler rode back into Colton, the pack mule trailing behind on its lead rope. He pulled off his hat and sleeved his arm across his forehead to remove the sweat. The day had unexpectedly turned hot. Dust from his horse's hoofs rose and tickled his nostrils. He pulled his hat back on, jerking the brim down to shade his face. He decided what he needed right now was a beer. Tessler preferred beer to spirits any day. A beer would go down nicely.

He let his horse pace itself along the rutted street until it reached the hitch rail outside the Colton Palace. It was one of the two saloons the town boasted. In Tessler's opinion, it was the better of the pair. He dismounted and secured his animals, took himself up on the boardwalk, and paused to look the town over. There were no more than a handful of people going about their business. Tessler allowed his gaze to linger on Pointer's store front and the jail next to it.

He wondered where Bodie was. The thought crossed his mind that maybe the manhunter had moved on; picked up where he had left off before running into the mustangers. If that was the case, then Tessler staying around Colton would prove to be a waste of time. Tessler decided he could follow the thought up after he'd had his glass of beer. Or two.

He made his way inside the saloon, dry hinges creaking as the batwings swung to and fro. Out of the sun, the interior took on a shady coolness. Tessler crossed to the long bar that dominated the right-hand side of the room. The open space left held a number of tables and chairs. At this time of the day, mid-afternoon, there were no more than a half dozen customers occupying the tables.

'Beer,' Tessler said to the stocky mustachioed bartender.

With the filled glass in front of him, Tessler took his time to imagine what it would taste like. Anticipation was often worth the time it took.

'You going to drink it, Tessler, or stare it to death?'

'Don't rush me, Quinn. I ain't a man to be herded when it comes to my beer.'

Quinn managed a smile and moved away to wipe the bar, leaving Tessler to his study of the amber liquid.

It was well over an hour later when Tessler exited the Colton Palace, his thirst well dusted down. Maybe too well dusted down, because true to his character, he had polished off a number of beers. One of his faults was he enjoyed his drinking too much, an inherent weakness that led him to indulge whenever the mood took him. Tessler had been working on the mustang trail for a few long weeks, and in the hills there was little chance to slake his thirst on anything except coffee or plain water. Being sent to town, albeit on a fact-finding mission, had let Tessler off the leash, away from Cabot and the restrictions imposed by long hours in the saddle, eating dust and breathing in the stink of wild horses. He had done his drinking on a near-empty stomach, which did nothing to reduce the effects of the alcohol. By the time he walked slowly from the saloon and out into the fresh air, Tessler was less than steady.

He paused on the edge of the boardwalk, a faint lightheadedness taking hold; yet Tessler was denying his slightly inebriated condition to himself. Like any man of his type, he always felt in control.

He took a moment to check the street, hitching his sagging gunbelt across his hips, settling the holster against his pants. The leather holster held the short-barreled .45 Colt Peacemaker he favored. The pistol had a set of wooden handles he had carved himself. They had a rough texture that increased his ability to achieve a solid grip when he drew. Claude Tessler relished his reputation as a shooter to be reckoned with. He had faced a number of opponents and had walked away from those encounters without a bullet coming near him. Tessler didn't openly brag about his skill. It was not in him. He knew he was good, and he didn't need anyone to tell him, and would not have welcomed it. As he stood on the boardwalk, Tessler's fingers freed the Colt's hammer loop, clearing it from the pistol.

He had been sent into Colton to find out what he could concerning Bodie. He had taken his drink, so now it was time to do just that. Refusing to accept he was not fully in control of himself, Tessler stepped awkwardly from the boardwalk and focused on the jail. He had a feeling Colton's lawman would be able to furnish him with any information regarding the bounty man. Be damned to what Cabot had said about not bracing the lawdog. Tessler didn't need instructions. He would find out Bodie's business in town and do it without wasting too much time. He hadn't quite figured out how he would broach the subject with Ezra Pointer, but he would think of something. Damn right he would.

He was partway along the street when Bodie appeared and started across. He moved steadily, favoring his sides, and Tessler was reminded of the beating the mustangers had given him. Served the sonofabitch right, asking too many questions that Cabot hadn't liked.

Tessler recalled the manhunter's stubborn refusal to back away when they had braced him back at the camp. Even when Cabot had warned him off, he had stood his ground and fought back like a wildcat, taking on four of them. He had gotten in a few good punches of his own before the mustangers took the high ground and put him down. Tessler reached up his left hand and touched the sore spot on his cheek where Bodie had caught him.

He stroked his fingers over the butt of his .45. This was as good a time as any to brace the man if he showed his face. He knew he could take him. Bodie was a bounty hunter, not a fast draw, and the lingering effects of the beating would have slowed him anyhow. If the man wasn't fast enough, that was his misfortune. Cabot wanted him out of his hair, so this was as good a time as any. All he had to do was call Bodie out and put him down for good.

The hell with Pointer. Tessler would go directly to the bounty man himself. There were a few people around to witness the event. Tessler would give Bodie fair warning, even give him a chance to go for his own gun to prove it was a fair fight.

'Bodie,' Tessler called.

4

He made his turn slowly, knowing a fast move would wrench at his sore ribs. The direct challenge in the single word told him this was no casual greeting. Coming around, he let his right hand slip easily to his side, level with the butt of the holstered Colt. The moment he laid eyes on the speaker, Bodie recognized him.

The one called Tessler from the mustangers' camp. Next to Cabot, he had been the main one who seemed to relish using his fists and boots. Bodie tamped down on the anger that threatened to rise. Yet he had a feeling to let his rage overwhelm him at the way the men in that camp had attacked him, but letting his emotions swamp his good sense right at this moment wasn't about to do him any favors. Facing a man who was intent on using his gun needed calm nerves and cool judgment. From the flushed look on Tessler's unshaven face, Bodie assumed the man was already wound up tight. Out of the corner of his eye, Bodie spotted a mule and horse hitched outside The Colton Palace. His guess would be that Tessler had spent some time in there. A drink, or a few, to combat the hot day before he walked out and spotted Bodie. That could account for the sweating face and the way Tessler rubbed his left hand across his dry mouth. His right hand hovered over the gun he wore, fingers flexing.

'Let it lie, feller. We had our go-around at your camp. No need to make more of it.'

'You damn well called us liars back there. We told you we didn't know anything about nobody called Trask.' Tessler thrust out his hand, finger jabbing in Bodie's direction. 'I figure that a downright insult, and I won't take that from any man.'

Now it was the drink talking. Bodie

picked up on the hint of a slur in Tessler's voice. 'I asked a question. You fellers were shy of telling the truth is all. You figure it's enough to go for a shooting match? Man would have to be a fool to do that.'

Tessler blinked as salty sweat trickled into his eyes. No matter what happened now, he was not about to back away. He *couldn't* back away. People were pausing along each side of the street, interest piqued as they watched. A shadow of doubt invaded Tessler's beer-induced nervousness. But he bridled at Bodie's suggestion that he was less than willing to speak the truth. Now he would have to show the bastard manhunter Claude Tessler could defend this personal insult.

'You called me a liar? Bad enough. Now you say I'm a fool. No man calls me that, Bodie. Especially a backshooting bounty hunter.'

'Tessler, you're facing me right now. Do you want me to turn away to give you a better chance?'

41

Tessler was at a loss, caught by a few words that had rebounded on him. 'The hell with you, Bodie. Let's do this.'

'It's the drink talking, Tessler. Go sleep it off before — '

Without even realizing how it was playing out, Claude Tessler went for his fast draw, fingers curling around his gun butt, feeling the textured grips against his flesh. In his wavering vision he saw Bodie standing motionless, too slow by far. Tessler's pistol cleared the holster, hammer being seared back as the weapon arced upwards.

He never saw Bodie's draw; missed the blur of motion as the manhunter's Colt rose and leveled, Bodie firing, cocking and firing again in a heartbeat.

Tessler felt a solid thump against his chest, then a second. The big lead slugs splintered rib bones and punctured his heart, the deformed bullets tearing the organ apart. He fell back, slamming to the ground hard, but barely felt the impact. His right hand opened and his unfired Colt slipped from his grasp.

The sudden silence that swept over Tessler was more terrifying than anything he had ever known. He saw the bright sky looming above him — yet it went from light to utter darkness so quickly Tessler had no time to wonder why.

*   *   *

'What happened here?' Pointer asked as he came out of his office, right hand clutching a pistol he had snatched from his desk drawer. He took in the scene at a glance: Bodie standing across the street, gun in his hand, facing in the direction of the man stretched out in the dirt. It was Claude Tessler, on his back, his drawn Colt in the dust close by. Tessler's hat lay a few feet away, moving as the slight breeze disturbed it.

A man close by said, 'Mustanger came out the saloon and braced the other feller. Wouldn't let it go, then went for his gun.'

'Seen it myself,' another said. 'Tessler

looked a little grieved about something. Way he acted, I'd say he'd been drinking some.'

A small crowd was gathering, drawn by the violence and the dead man — instinctive curiosity that was always revealed. Bodie put his gun away and walked over to where Pointer stood. The lawman stared at him, trying to understand the suddenness of what had happened. He was a part-time official, and the kind of violence that had just visited Colton was beyond his remit.

'Better get something to cover the body,' Bodie said. 'Don't want women or kids to see it.'

Pointer nodded and looked around, picking someone from the gathering crowd. 'Jonas, go tell Brinkerman there's a body needs tending. Ask him to deal with it soon as.'

A lean towheaded young man in a dark suit, clutching a dangling tailor's tape measure in one hand, drew his gaze from the body and started up the street.

Pointer's wife appeared, a folded sheet in her hands, and with her husband's help she covered the body. 'Are you hurt, Mister Bodie?' she asked.

'No, ma'am, but thanks for asking.'

'I saw what happened from the store window. Why was that man so angry with you?'

'He had a notion I'd slighted him and was bound and determined to put it to rights.'

'By making you fight over it? Was it worth losing his life for?'

'Jen, it's done,' Pointer said quietly. 'I doubt Mister Bodie wanted it to happen so.'

Mister Bodie, notwithstanding the circumstances, might have thought differently but said nothing. He walked in a different world than the one Jen Pointer inhabited. The sudden and merciless violence he experienced had no place in her ordered existence; and even if he sat down and tried to explain it, she would not have understood.

Claude Tessler, however, would have no problem in the telling. He had lived in the uncompromising place that paralleled Bodie's own. The harsh reality of their lives was accepted. It had become the norm, and they took the knocks that came with it.

'Pointer, I'll move on come morning,' Bodie said. 'Last thing you need is me drawing any more problems your way.'

'There's no need for that. Bodie, this man here came looking for you with the intention of causing trouble. I regret he had to die, but I don't hold you responsible. From what I've heard, you had little choice. You simply defended yourself.'

'And if any more of Will Cabot's men come to town? If the same thing happens and an innocent party is involved?'

Pointer became aware of the gun still dangling from his hand. He quickly tucked it behind his belt. 'Four years I've been part-time marshal. Never fired a weapon in all those years.' He gave a soft laugh. 'Damned if I'd know what to do if the time came.'

'You'd do what was needed. I'd better go and have that meal I was planning on, then I'll get some rest. I'll ride out at first light. See if I can pick up on Trask's trail again.'

Bodie nodded in Jen Pointer's direction and turned about, heading for the restaurant just along the street.

5

Bodie had learned a long time back that eating well before a long trek was a good habit to acquire. Leaving Colton would put him on a trail that might easily take him into lonely country, where food and drink would only come from what a man was able to carry with him. There was only so much he would be able to pack along; and depending on local weather conditions, cooking a meal might not be so easy. So Bodie took himself a table in Monty's Restaurant. He ordered a big steak with all the trimmings and a pot of fresh coffee to go with.

Monty turned out to be a handsome middle-aged woman who appeared to have full knowledge of Bodie's business in town. Within a minute of sitting down, she placed a mug of steaming coffee in front of him and took his order, passing it through to the kitchen. Bodie had just sampled the coffee when the woman showed up again, an inquiring look on her face.

'Can I take a guess that what happened out there is not your first time, Mister Bodie?'

'Now that's a direct way of saying hello.'

'I have no toleration of time-wasting chatter. That man, Tessler, made it his intention to push you into a gunfight.'

'Yes he did, ma'am.'

She studied the bruising marks on his face and the way he sat stiffly, favoring his sides. 'He have anything to do with your injuries?'

'He was involved.'

'Will Cabot's crew?'

'Yes'm.'

'You would have been well advised to stay well clear of those mustangers.'

'Too late now.'

'Mister Bodie, I declare you are a man of few words.'

'Coffee's good.'

She laughed at that. An honest, husky sound that filled the room.

'Monty?'

'My late departed husband was Roman Montefiore. So I became Lucinda Montefiore. Never liked Lucinda, and I kind of took to Monty when Roman called me that. I let it stay out of respect.'

In the pause that followed, Bodie decided the name suited the woman. 'You have this place when he was alive?'

'We did. When we came here, Colton was just getting established. Roman loved to cook. And he was good at it. He knew that where people gathered, they would need a place to eat. The town. The outlying ranches. Passing trade.' She hesitated. 'I wouldn't know what else to do, Bodie. It's my life. And you, Bodie — is what you do your life?'

'I guess so. We all find the path best suited to us.'

'Profound.'

'Coming from a bounty hunter, you mean.'

'I wasn't talking down to you. I just figure there's more to your story. What were you before you took to chasing down men?'

'A US Marshal.'

'You gave up that life? There must have been a good reason.'

This time he simply nodded. A teenage girl emerged from the kitchen, carrying a tray that held Bodie's food. The plate she set down was loaded with a large steak, browned potatoes and vegetables. A jug of rich gravy and a side plate of hot biscuits followed.

'If it tastes as good as it looks, no wonder this place is so popular.'

Monty smiled. 'Tell all your friends.'

Bodie held her gaze. 'Friends?'

In that single word, Monty understand a part of what made up Bodie's life. He was a man always on the move. His trade as a hunter of men made him a loner, traveling from place to place and seeking out the fugitives of society. Not a profession that would endear him to many, and most likely bring out the worst in some. Thinking on that made her wonder why he stayed with it, placing himself in danger. As an occupation, being a bounty hunter offered little in recompense; just the hardship and the distancing from much of polite society.

'This man you're following,' Monty asked, 'is there a connection to Will Cabot and his mustangers?'

'I just asked if they knew his whereabouts,' Bodie said. 'It got me a beating.' He managed a wry smile. 'And I still don't know why. Yet.'

'Tessler took it badly?'

'Feller figured I'd slighted him. Kind of touched a raw nerve.'

'But to die for it?'

'Fine line between an insult and a man's pride.'

'Pride?'

'Times are, that's all a man has. It's important to him.'

'The man is dead, Bodie. He died for nothing.'

'Yes, ma'am.'

'And this man you're chasing — do the same rules apply? Wanted dead or alive?'

'I work by what the law dictates. That's the way it is, ma'am.'

'Sounds so cut and dried, Mister Bodie. And convenient.'

Bodie caught the bitter tone in her voice before she checked herself and made an awkward sweep of her hand over her hair, brushing it back from her face. He kept his eyes on his plate, concentrating on the food.

Monty stood for a moment, looking down at him. Her hands at her sides were clenched into tight fists. Bodie sensed a deal of tension there and found himself wondering why.

'I should let you finish your meal in peace, Mister Bodie. Excuse my outburst. I must still be upset after the shooting. It isn't something that happens a lot in Colton.'

She turned away suddenly, crossing the restaurant, and disappeared in the kitchen. Bodie watched her go, trying to figure out the change of mood. He decided to let it go and concentrated on his steak, which was turning out to be good. He finished his meal and emptied the coffee pot. After he paid the young waitress, he left the restaurant and made his way to the boarding house Pointer had recommended, getting directions from people he asked.

It turned out to be a two-story white-painted house standing behind a picket fence and a tidy piece of garden. As Bodie took himself to the steps leading to the verandah, the house door opened and a stern-faced woman in her fifties stepped out, regarding him soberly. Her hands crossed in front of her as she watched Bodie in silence.

He took off his hat. 'Mrs. Toliver? The marshal told me — '

'I have your room ready, Mister Bodie. I hope you'll not be wearing that weapon inside my house.'

Bodie removed his rig and coiled it up. 'No, ma'am.'

'Thank you for that.' There was a

pained expression on her face as she took in his travel-stained clothing. 'Have you any clean things to wear, Mister Bodie?'

'My gear is down at the livery. I can go get it.'

'No need. I'll send Obadiah.' Her manner changed and she looked him over. 'Ezra said you'd been hurt. From the way you walk, I'd say he wasn't exaggerating.'

'Doc Meerschaum tended to me.'

'Yes; I can smell that infernal liniment he favors.' The hint of a smile touched her pale lips. 'Truth be told, it does smell, but it has powerful properties.'

She led the way inside, and Bodie followed her along the neat passage. There were pictures on the walls, doors leading off on either side. He could hear a clock ticking somewhere. A neat and orderly house, just like Mrs. Toliver. She pushed a door open to reveal a sunlit room that held a bed and furniture. On a small table by the window was an ornate oil lamp.

'There's a bathroom two doors along. Privy is out back. I can have Obadiah heat some water so you can wash when he gets back from the livery with your belongings. Will the room be suitable?'

Bodie put his wrapped gunrig aside and covered it with his hat. 'Ma'am, it's more than suitable. I'm grateful for your hospitality.'

'The marshal tells me you had little choice in the matter when that man challenged you.'

'I could've walked away, but my feeling was if I did I would've given him an easier target. Don't know how else I could have handled it. He wasn't agreeable to talking it out.'

Bodie had a restless night, sleep hard coming due to his sore ribs. He found it difficult to settle. He slept eventually, and when he rose, Mrs. Toliver prepared him a good breakfast. Later he made his way to the stable, saddled the chestnut and secured his supplies. It

was a warm morning when he called by
the store and spoke briefly to Pointer
before taking his leave of Colton.

6

Bodie traversed the steep slope, letting his horse pick its way over the uneven ground. He sat easy in his saddle, still conscious of the tender condition of his ribs. His face was still sore, so he passed on trying to shave. He was determined not to allow his physical condition cause him to lose his concentration. He had found the faint tracks left by Trask and was hell bent on not losing them.

Tracking the man was turning out to be easier than he might have expected. Trask was not making any attempt to hide his trail, most likely intent on making time and distance against anyone following him. It made no real sense. And because of that, Bodie was concerned. A running man might be lax in his efforts to hide where he was going, but even the most desperate would make some attempt to cover his back trail.

'Horse, I don't like the way this is stringing out,' Bodie said. 'It's like he doesn't care if he's followed.'

The powerful chestnut, used to picking up its rider's verbal comments, simply dipped its head and gave a low nicker.

'You're a great help.'

He heeled the chestnut forward, still conscious of the nagging doubt in his mind. It was that doubt that made him lean forward to slide the rifle from the saddle boot.

And that move drew him clear of the slug coming from behind. He felt the ripple of it passing him close, then kicked his feet free from the stirrups and rolled off the horse. He managed to keep his feet under him as he landed, dropping to a crouch and bringing the Winchester into play. He bit back the surge of pain from his ribs as the impact of his sudden move disturbed them.

Bodie heard a second shot. The slug kicked up a gout of dirt a couple of feet to his left. Grit peppered his legs. He spotted a dip in the ground and slid into it, twisting over onto his stomach and searched in the direction of the shooter. He saw a fading drift of powder smoke coming from a clump of brush. His sighting was confirmed when a third shot came, the hard crash of the weapon echoing across the slopes. His ambusher was using a rifle. Confirming that didn't ease Bodie's situation any.

He heard the thump of the chestnut's hoofs as the animal moved away, and stayed motionless and waited. He had the shooter's position marked now, and though he hadn't yet been able to see him in amongst the close vegetation, he knew he would be able to spot him if the man made to change position. Bodie's rifle rested on the lip of the depression, butt against his shoulder and his finger hovering over the trigger.

Come on, you son of a bitch. Show yourself.

It happened a couple of minutes later when the brush was disturbed, and the manhunter's patience was rewarded by a dark bulk easing to one side. Light flickered off the barrel of a rifle — only briefly, but enough to give Bodie his target. He took a breath, held it, and led his target before stroking back on the rifle's light trigger. He felt the Winchester kick back, then levered and fired again. The shots were loud in his ears.

A man cried out. There was a thrashing movement in the brush.

Bodie pushed to his feet, this time ignoring the pain in his ribs as he cut across the slope. He came on the clump of brush from the side and picked up the groans coming from the heart of the brush.

The shooter was hunched over, his dark-clad legs pulled up almost to his chest in obvious agony. His hands were clutching at the bloody wounds high up on his chest where Bodie's slugs had hit off to the left side and due to the short range had gone all the way through and exited his shoulder, leaving behind large ragged wounds. Blood was flowing from both sides of his body, already having soaked his buckskin shirt in excess.

The man was moaning in a continuous high-pitched voice, the sound grating on Bodie's nerves. He bent over and cleared away the man's dropped rifle and the .44 caliber pistol in the holster. The man twisted his head round to stare up at Bodie, who didn't recognize him. He had a pinched face with pocked skin and a straggly sandy mustache. He had lost his hat, exposing a bald skull.

'I'll bet that hurts something awful,' Bodie said.

The man stared at him. Tears were running from his screwed-up eyes, leaving pale tracks in his dirt-smeared cheeks. 'I nearly had you there, pilgrim,' the man whispered.

'Nearly ain't good enough,' Bodie said. 'You feel like telling me why?'

'Gold pieces in my pocket. That do?'

'Damn shame you won't get to spend them.'

The man didn't reply, and when Bodie checked, he was unconscious. Blood was still coming from the wounds in copious amounts. The man's breathing was shallow. Bodie understood the signs. The loss of blood was becoming too much. He was close to death. It would have taken the skill of someone like Doc Meerschaum to keep him alive, and even he would have struggled. The man had taken money with the intention of shooting the manhunter — in the back as well; and that annoyed him.

Bodie crossed to where the man had been concealed. Thirty feet further back in the brush, he found his horse and led it back to where the unconscious man lay. He stripped off the saddle and trappings and swatted the horse on the rump, setting it free, then took the man's blanket roll and slid it under his head. Bodie felt his eyes on him.

'Thanks. Name's Dorn . . . Linus Dorn.'

'Don't mean we get to hold hands in the moonlight,' Bodie said.

'I made a mess of it,' Dorn said, his voice hushed. 'Shouldn't have let that woman talk me into it. She made it sound like easy money . . . '

Bodie felt a shiver of expectation crawl the length of his backbone. 'Monty,' he said. Not a question. More a statement of fact.

'Monty,' Dorn said. 'Hell of a name for a woman. Don't you . . . ' His voice trailed away, fading to silence. And he was dead.

Bodie removed the blanket roll from under Dorn's head and shook it out, then draped the blankets over the body, covering the face. He pushed to his feet and raised his eyes to view the rise of the high slopes. The sun was stronger now on his face.

'Monty,' he said. He walked to where his horse stood waiting, mounted up, and picked up the faint trail again.

* * *

Late in the afternoon, Bodie turned in his saddle and saw three riders briefly outlined against the sky. They rode into a dip and vanished, but he knew they were still coming in his direction. He figured they were two miles behind, and the landscape would hold them back from making a fast ride.

He also had a feeling he knew who they were: Cabot's mustangers, on his trail and making no attempt to hide from him. It seemed Will Cabot was full intentioned on forcing Bodie's hand.

While he rode, checking the way ahead, Bodie had plenty of time to think; to try and work out the whole damned mess. Because that was how it seemed to him. There was Sam Trask, the man who had brought Bodie to the Dakotas. A wanted man on the run, accused of rape and murder, who had killed the coach driver even though he had left Eli Pruitt alone. Now Will Cabot and his mustanger crew. There had to be a connection between Cabot and the fugitive. A connection Bodie needed to find.

And now the paid gunman sent out after him by the woman called Monty. He had only met her the once in her restaurant, and now she was sending out a hired gun to kill him. Thinking about her brought back the way she had acted on the matter of Bodie going after a wanted man.

He figured there had to be a thread in the mix, one thing that linked everything together. But he wasn't going to solve it while he had a sorry bunch of individuals on his ass, and none of them offering much in the way of comfort.

Would Sam Trask be able to offer a key to the puzzle? It was a possibility, though with the way the man was acting, Bodie had his doubts.

He realized he could be expecting too much from Trask. Maybe the man had no idea how much interest he was creating by going on the run.

★ ★ ★

Bodie was topping yet another ridgeline. He reined in to allow his chestnut to take a rest. The horse had carried him all this way without complaint, and Bodie felt guilty. It wasn't as if he had been hard riding — far from it; but the sheer strain of climbing the Dakota high country must have placed a great deal of pressure on the mare. So he slid from the saddle, loosened the cinch, and tipped water from one of his big canteens into his upturned hat, allowing the horse to drink. When it had slaked its thirst, he shucked out the remaining drops of water and hung it from his saddlehorn, letting the warm sun start to dry it out. He took a drink himself before hooking the canteen strap back in place.

While the chestnut took time to crop the grass around them, Bodie scanned the way ahead and in every other direction. Over the last few hours, the thin trail had led him ever higher, but

Bodie didn't forget the trio of riders he'd seen earlier. There had been no sign of them since. Either they had realized they had been spotted and were keeping out of sight, or they were drawing closer and awaiting their chances.

Chances to do what? Gun him down? Capture him?

Bodie breathed in the clean air. It was fresher up here on the higher slopes. Despite the sun, there was a noticeable coolness there. The high altitude would most likely turn the air colder as the afternoon wore on. Once the sun set, the hill country would rapidly lose the daylong heat and the temperature would drop. Here in the Dakota high country, the climate could change with unexpected swiftness. When it did, the results could be severe and extreme in some cases.

In January 1888, the so-called Schoolchildren's Blizzard had killed 235 people, many of whom were children on their way home from school. The bitter powdered snow spread across the northwest plains region of the United States. It had come without warning, and it was said that the temperature fell nearly 100 degrees in one day. It was a Thursday afternoon, and there had been unseasonably warm weather the previous day from Montana across to the Dakotas, even as far as Texas. Suddenly, within a few of hours, arctic air from Canada swept south. Temperatures plunged to 40 below zero in much of Northern Dakota. Along with the cool air, the storm brought high winds and the unstoppable blinding snow. The combination created terrible conditions. There was nothing anyone could do to prevent it, or hope to resist its grip. In this high country, due to its position, severe weather could set in quickly, and there was little that could be done to prevent it. It was nature's way to be unpredictable, and for all his cleverness, man had no chance when it decided to strike.

Bodie checked his holstered Colt to confirm it was fully loaded, then did the same with the rifle in the saddle boot. He was simply taking precautions, rather than feeling paranoid; an instinct born from having stayed alive so long by always making sure his available weapons were primed and ready for use.

He found that the tracks he was following led along the ridgeline, and picking up the chestnut's rein he walked it in that direction. Although the ridge had a rocky stratum beneath the grass and mossy patches, Bodie had no trouble keeping the hoof prints in sight. Having followed them for some time now, he was able to recognize the shape, so he knew he was following the right man. The slopes he had ridden were dotted with stands of timber: a varied mix of aspen, oak and birch. Further north, the timbered tracts grew thicker, interspersed with brush and swaths of grass. Bodie picked out the gleam of meandering streams coming down from the higher reaches of the hills. It was good-looking country — maybe isolated, but that at least meant it was still mainly uninhabited. He wondered if that was because the area was way off the regular trails, or had not yet had its natural potential realized.

'Take a good look, horse. Come the day, it'll change.' The chestnut lifted her head at the sound of his voice. 'Time you earned your keep.'

Bodie tightened the saddle, gathered the reins and mounted up. He turned the horse and put it along the line of hoof prints. Something told him he was about to ride higher, taking himself to the uppermost point of this section.

Bodie had his eyes above the top peaks and scanned the open sky. Gray cloud formations were moving in his direction. They had that heavy look that held the threat of rain. It was nothing surprising for this far north and the altitude.

Now Bodie never welcomed rain. In

most cases it was cold; and, stating the obvious, it was wet. Whether it was gentle spring rain, or downright vicious, he had an aversion to it. Up on these open slopes it would come in with a chill and heavy hand, so Bodie unfurled the oilskin slicker from his blanket roll and shook it out. He draped it across the rear skirt of his saddle, there for fast retrieval if — no, when, he corrected — he needed it.

Overshadowing his personal objection to the rain was the certain knowledge that any prolonged downpour could easily wipe away the thin trail he was following. He pushed the chestnut on a little faster, his eyes fixed on the tracks.

Twenty minutes later, he felt the first raindrops coming in at an angle that indicated they were being driven by the breeze from the higher peaks. Over the next few minutes, the opening spatter grew. Bodie felt the increasingly larger drops were coming at a faster rate. A sudden gust of wind slapped the rain into his face. It was cold, and stung the tender bruises still showing. Thinking about the bruises concentrated his attention on his ribs. The dull ache was still there, reminding him what had happened. Doc Meerschaum had warned him about doing anything too strenuous. The hours he had since spent in the saddle were making themselves known.

He halted, dragged the slicker from behind the saddle, and pulled it on over his head. The dark clouds were pushing in faster now, and he could see they would be overhead in a short time.

Bodie sighed. There was nothing he could do but stay on line. Trask appeared to be continuing north. The ride towards the border, and Canada seemed more than ever the man's destination. So Bodie stayed on the same course.

7

Charbonneau pushed to his feet and nodded at his partners. 'It's him. Linus Dorn. Looks like a couple of shots. Must have hit hard, and he bled to death.'

Kellin shrugged. 'Amateur.'

Jay Kellin, although a mustanger, sported a cared-for Remington pistol. He had a reputation as a man to be reckoned with when it came to using the weapon. He didn't feel the need to have to go around boasting about his skill. Kellin let his gun prove his point.

'Cabot wants this Bodie feller putting down. That's why he sent us,' the third man said. His name was Royster. A cold-eyed individual who wore a buckskin outfit and a coonskin hat, he seldom asked for anything, and certainly did not give anything away. He had no sidearm, but simply carried a

Henry repeating rifle and was no slouch when it came to using it. On the broad belt he wore hung a war hatchet he had taken from a Sioux warrior he had killed many years ago. On his other hip was a sheathed knife. It was said Royster enjoyed the act of killing a little too much, but no one would ever say it in hearing distance.

'This feller, Bodie — it don't call to mess around with him. The man has proved his worth plenty,' Charbonneau said. 'I've heard the stories about him.'

'A bullet will cut him down same as any other man,' Royster stated.

Rain was falling now, hissing down from a clouded sky. None of the three paid any attention to it. They were well used to the variable weather of the high country and were not about to allow it to put them off what they had to do.

Back in the saddle, Charbonneau swung his shaggy mustang back on the trail, and the three moved off.

The man called Bodie was ahead of them. They were closing on him, familiar with the mountain trails, and they figured they would make contact before dark.

Sooner or later they would be close enough to take on the manhunter.

8

The temperature had fallen. The wind coming down out of Canada brought an icy blast with it. Bodie felt it through the slicker, and the touch of it against his bruised face made him flinch. Even though he had pulled on a pair of leather gloves, his hands were starting to become numb. Sheeting rain hit him time after time, rocking him in the saddle. He couldn't recall the last time he had felt so cold.

He was starting to believe he had lost the trail. The ground was awash, and any hoof prints, faint as they might have been, were about to be sluiced out of existence by the relentless downpour.

'Seems to me, horse, we could be on a loser here.'

The plodding gait of the chestnut faltered. She came to a stop, not even raising her head, and Bodie could understand the animal's mood. He leaned forward and stroked her neck. When he sat upright, he saw the shape of the building some way off to his right. It was a solid timber structure with corrals and stable at the side. Bodie sat and examined it, feeling at first he was imagining it. Then he caught the scraps of smoke rising from the stone chimney. The curls of gray whipped away by the wind as they emerged.

'I can feel my luck changing,' he said.

He pulled on the reins and guided the chestnut down the gentle slope in front of them. He saw that a large area fronting the building had been cleared of trees and scrub, leaving a generous open space. The clearing had plainly been done some time in the past, because the exposed tree stumps looked weathered.

On impulse, Bodie slid his right hand under the slicker and gripped the holstered Colt. His gaze moved restlessly back and forth, checking and rechecking. There was no movement. He saw the windows flanking each side of the main door. The rain bounced off real glass in the frames. Someone had gone to a great deal of trouble hauling it all the way up here. The construction of the building had been carried out with a thought for permanence. The solid logs used had been well fitted and measured to within an inch, and the door suggested it was there to stay. Bodie found himself wondering who had gone to so much trouble, and why.

'Let's go find out.'

A flicker of movement on the far side of the corral caught Bodie's eye — a slight figure enveloped in a black slicker that looked too big for whoever wore it. Bodie saw a pale face peering at him from the sodden hat pulled low. It was a young woman, eyes wide with alarm when she saw Bodie's mounted bulk staring down at her.

'Be obliged if I could put my horse under cover, ma'am. Weather kind of came fast.'

'Go ahead,' she said. Her voice was firm as she recovered from her initial surprise. 'There's plenty of room.'

She turned and retraced her steps to the stable to one side of the corral. By the time Bodie reached the structure, she had a door pulled back. He eased the chestnut inside, the interior warm-smelling and out of the storm. He swung out of the saddle, sensing the young woman close behind, watching him.

Bodie counted at least six stalled horses. He led the chestnut to an empty one, stripped off saddle and trappings, and tethered the horse. Without a word, the young woman forked in fresh straw and topped up the feed trough with oats. Bodie used the saddle blanket to wipe down the chestnut's wet body, then hung it over the side of the stall alongside his saddle.

'Says a lot about a man who looks after his animal,' the young woman said. She dragged off the rain-sodden hat, a thick fall of red hair tumbling free. She regarded Bodie with bright hazel eyes full of curiosity and confidence.

'That lady has done good work today,' Bodie said. 'Brought me all the way up here from Colton. Have to say I welcomed the sight of this place.'

'I'm Jessie Gibbs,' the young woman said. 'This is my father's place. Isaac Gibbs.'

'Bodie.'

'Will you come inside, Mister Bodie? There's hot coffee on the go and a fire to ward off the chills.'

'Sounds good.' He gathered his saddlebags and rifle and followed Jessie from the barn to the house. She pushed open the heavy door and led the way inside.

'Dad, we have another visitor. This is Mister Bodie.'

Isaac Gibbs had red hair like his daughter. It was the only thing they seemed to have in common. Where she was slim and almost petite, her father was a giant of a man, well over six feet with wide, powerful shoulders. He sported a neatly trimmed beard and possessed huge hands, his left gripping the carved crutch that relieved the pressure on his left leg, which was splinted and bandaged. The dark pants he wore had the left leg split around the injured limb. Despite this and his size, the man moved with ease as he crossed to greet Bodie, holding out his ham-like right hand. Bodie felt the latent strength in Gibbs's big hand.

'Go warm yourself at the fire, Mister Bodie.'

Bodie peeled off his slicker and hung it from a wooden peg next to the door. Jessie took his hat and saddlebags, leaving him with the Winchester. He propped it up against the wall and walked across the wide room to stand in the throw of heat from the generous stone fireplace, where thick logs burned steadily.

Jessie took off her own slicker, hung it, then crossed the room to attend to the coffee pot standing on a cast-iron support in the open fireplace. She poured the steaming brew into a thick china mug and handed it to Bodie. With the slicker off, he could see she was clad in a check shirt and denim dungarees, with solid leather boots on her feet.

'We can go for weeks without seeing a new face,' Isaac Gibbs said. 'Now we get two of them.'

Movement on the far side of the room caught Bodie's attention. A dark figure sitting in a shadowed corner stood and eased forward. Light spilled across his face. Bodie watched the man over the rim of the coffee mug. He recognized the face straight off. The last time he had seen it had been on the wanted flyer Ed Pruitt had shown him.

It was the fugitive Bodie was trailing up the mountain slopes.

Sam Trask.

9

They had taken shelter in the protection of a wide overhang and waited out the worst of the rainstorm. None of them was particularly happy over the change in the weather and the effect it was having on their pursuit of Bodie.

'He could be over the border by now,' Royster grumbled. 'Him and Trask. That's who he's after. We know that and so does Cabot.'

Charbonneau pulled his slicker tighter around him. He was angry at having to delay their pursuit. It had been forced on them by the storm's increased ferocity. Trying to keep moving had become nigh impossible, and Charbonneau had made the decision to halt at least for a while. He had decided it was too risky to keep moving and be damned to what Cabot expected. There were times Cabot expected too much. A man's life was not worth risking for someone like Sam Trask.

Just because Cabot ramrodded the mustangers, he imagined his word was never to be challenged. Being the boss man had taken over his thinking. In the case of Sam Trask, it was bordering on lunacy in Charbonneau's eyes. Ever since Trask had shown up, Cabot had been acting strange, like nothing else mattered. Charbonneau couldn't avoid thinking about that — the way Cabot was doing whatever he could to protect the man.

He had made it clear to the mustangers that they should leave Trask alone while the man had been in camp — not question him or have anything to do with him. And they obeyed, as Cabot was not a man to cross. He could change moods in an instant, and Will Cabot losing control was not a sight any of them wanted to see. He was also their boss; their employer. He kept them in work and paid their wages, and they were all beholden to him for that. Not a man in the crew wanted to go against him. It had happened a couple of times in the past. They all recalled what had been the result. Taking all those things into consideration, they did as they were ordered and carried on with their work. Chasing the herds of wild mustangs across the Dakota hills was enough to keep any man occupied. It was back-breaking dirty work. So Cabot's crew put their efforts into that and left the rest alone.

And when you took a man's wages and rode for the brand, it was an unspoken law that made you side with him. If you didn't, it was a betrayal of loyalty.

Charbonneau had been with Cabot for a long time, working the wild horse roundups and providing a handy gun when needed. The mustang business was tough, and rival crews competed for the best herds. It sometimes came to open disputes; and when that occurred, it was Charbonneau who settled them. He was known as a man who tolerated no nonsense. Men who stood up to him had cause to regret their rash actions. Charbonneau never made threats he was not prepared to carry out. He carried a .45 Peacemaker in a cutaway holster on his left hip, and when he drew it, it was not to show it off. Charbonneau only took out his gun when he was about to use it. And he always shot to kill, never to wound; because a wounded man, like an injured predator, might still have it in him to continue the fight. Charbonneau had seen that happen, and early on he had reached the decision it would never happen to him. So far that philosophy had kept him alive, and he had no inclination to change it. Once a man was dead, that was the end of it all. No second chance. No comeback. So putting off a premature end to life had become an important consideration.

Royster, rolling himself a smoke from where he leaned against the rock, said,

'How'd we get talked into this? Riding these damned hills looking for that feller, Bodie. Hey, Charbonneau, you're the brains of this outfit. How'd we get the short straw?'

'We're lucky, I guess,' Kellin said.

'Somethin' tells me luck had nothing to do with it.' Royster struck a match on the rock face and lit his quirly, sucking the bitter smoke deep into his lungs. 'So what you say, Charbonneau?'

'You keep smoking the way you do, your lungs will be full of soot,' Charbonneau said, staring across at Royster from beneath the wide brim of his hat. 'We got the job, so quit bellyaching and enjoy the view.'

Royster shook his head. Sometimes there was no getting a straight answer from Charbonneau. The man could be downright impossible to figure. He looked across at Kellin, but his partner simply gave a shrug. He was happy to do whatever Charbonneau told him; content to do whatever he was told; draw his pay and ride on. There were times Royster envied Kellin's uncomplicated attitude.

'Ain't that Gibbs's place up this way?' Kellin asked. 'Pretty sure it is. Be a way north of us. Mebbe that Bodie hombre went there and took shelter hisself.'

'Could be,' Charbonneau said. 'Worth takin' a look.'

Kellin sucked on his cigarette. 'I got that right.' He looked across at Royster. 'Seems as I ain't as dumb as you figure, Royster.'

'Hell, Kellin, nobody could be that dumb an' still be walking around.'

Kellin simply grinned. He and Royster had an ongoing line of insulting each other that went back a long way. They had been saddle partners before tying up with Cabot, and their sparring never seemed to end. The more it seemed to annoy their companions, the more they indulged.

'Being stuck out here with you two is worse than a ten-year sentence in Yuma Pen,' Charbonneau said.

Silence reigned for a time before Royster said, 'There'd be hot coffee on offer at Gibbs's place.'

'Sounds tempting,' Kellin agreed. 'Charbonneau?'

Charbonneau had seen the rain slacking off. He checked his horse and swung into the saddle. 'Let's ride,' he said. 'Anything's better than listening to you nattering like a pair of old ladies.'

10

Bodie moved his gaze from Trask across to Isaac Gibbs. He had showed no facial reaction on recognizing the fugitive. It was not the time.

'Bust your leg?' he asked, keeping his tone neutral.

Gibbs gave an embarrassed laugh. 'You'd think at my age I'd take more care. Did it falling out of the loft in the stable. Damn fool thing to do.'

Jessie said, 'He has to prove he's still able to do things he could when he was twenty years younger.'

'She likes to mother me,' Gibbs said.

'With good reason.'

Gibbs lowered his bulk into a solid armchair and stretched his splinted leg out in front of him. Jessie brought him a mug of coffee.

Sam Trask had moved forward, holding out his own mug. 'Be obliged for a refill, Miss Gibbs.'

Jessie poured for him. 'Oh, this is Mister Bodie,' she said. 'Another refugee from the storm. Mister Bodie, this is Mister Lester Kincaid.'

Bodie gave a brief nod.

'And there I was thinking I was the only one foolish enough to go out in the storm,' Trask said.

His voice was quiet, pleasant enough, yet Bodie detected a hint of something cold behind the words. Trask moved closer to the fire. Even though he wore thick pants and shirt, with a long dark topcoat, he appeared to feel the chill. Firelight glanced off his face, showing the strong bone formation. When he moved, it was with deliberate awareness. The man was showing himself as easygoing, with no hidden agenda. Bodie thought otherwise. This was the man he had come looking for. The one who carried a flyer on him that said Trask was wanted for rape and murder, among other things.

'What brings you all the way up

here?' Trask asked.

'Passing through,' Bodie said. 'Kind of got off my trail when the weather hit.'

'Heading for?'

'Way west. I heard out in California the weather's passing fair.'

'Mister Bodie, you're well off your trail,' Isaac Gibbs said.

'I kind of figured that.'

'Well, you can wait out the storm here,' Jessie said. 'Just like Mister Kincaid.'

Bodie nodded. 'Grateful for that.'

Out the corner of his eye, Bodie saw Trask's expression harden. He didn't appear too happy about the arrangement. Bodie decided he was going to need to stay alert. His senses told him Trask might have other plans. He had gotten this far, and it didn't seem likely he was ready to give up now. If he suspected Bodie was more than he was claiming . . .

Bodie didn't want Isaac Gibbs and his daughter placed in any firing line if it came to that. The problem with that suggested Trask might have other ideas.

11

'I seen him,' Royster yelled. 'Over to the stable. He come out the house and crossed over.'

He ran forward, rifle up and suddenly firing. He loosed off a rapid volley that did little except punch holes in the swinging door.

'That boy just likes to make a deal of noise,' Charbonneau said. 'Kellin, get around the back.'

Kellin spurred his horse into motion, yanking on the reins to swing it down the side of the stable, muddy soil spraying from under its pounding hoofs. Reaching the far corner of the stable, he flung himself from the saddle, Remington in his hand, and angled it in the direction of the rear door. He reached out to drag the door open. The sound of more shots reached him from the front of the stable. Kellin moved forward as soon as there was enough room to slip through. It was dimmer inside the stable, yet there was enough light for him to be able to see the layout. He saw horses in the stalls, restless as they reacted to the shooting. He gripped the pistol, scanning the interior.

'Bodie, we got you cornered, so give it up.'

Kellin saw movement close by one of the stalls. The tall figure of the bounty man stepped into view, Winchester in his hands.

'Just remember you came after me.'

Kellin had no chance to reply. The rifle thundered out a number of shots, the .44–40 slugs hammering into his chest and knocking him on his back. He slammed to the stable floor, echoes of the shots the last thing he heard.

★ ★ ★

Bodie had finished his coffee, made small talk for a while, then said he wanted to make sure his horse was settled for the rest of the stay. He pulled on his slicker and hat and took his rifle as he stepped out of the house, feeling the slap of the rain the moment he moved clear. Behind him, Jessie called for him not to be long because food would be served soon. Crossing the yard, he bent his head against the driving rain and eased inside the stable.

He had used his excuse about the chestnut to get himself out of the house, his intention to work his way around the building and come up behind Trask by way of the kitchen. He had seen the back door during a casual glance around the interior. It wasn't much of a plan, but he figured it was going to be the best he could work up at the moment.

★ ★ ★

With Kellin down, Bodie reminded himself there were three of them.

He turned about as he heard the

creak of the stable main door. A hand showed, pistol leading, and shots were fired. The stalled horses began to panic, shrilling their fear as the shots sounded.

Bodie crouched, shouldering the rifle, and put a fast trio of shots into the door where he figured the hidden shooter was standing. He saw wood splinters explode as the slugs tore through the door. He heard a man gasp, then saw the door sway as a weight fell against it. A bloodied figure fell across the opening, punctured by Bodie's slugs. It was Royster, rifle slipping from his hands as he dropped.

Two down. That left the one called Charbonneau.

Bodie remembered him from the mustangers' camp; one of the men who had been at the forefront of the attackers. His aching ribs chose that moment to offer a surge of pain that made him aware of his situation. He listened to the hiss of the falling rain. It was liable to mask any movement the man might make. Kellin and Royster had made their physical presence known, and it had made Bodie's task easier. He had a feeling Charbonneau wasn't about to do anything as casual.

He leaned forward and pushed at the closest of the stable doors; let it swing wide and open up the yard. He stayed to the side where he could see but not be seen himself. The yard was empty save for three horses hitched beside the corral. They stood close together, heads lowered. The rain was still coming down in silvery sheets, buffeted by the wind. The exposed yard already held pools of water. Bodie threw a quick glance in the direction of the house. There was no movement he could see behind the windows. Where was Charbonneau?

It was an easy enough question. All Bodie wanted was an easy answer. That was where life refused to play along. It had the habit of putting a man's back to the wall and leaving him to face his difficulties in the dark.

He checked the Winchester. There

should still be plenty of shots left, and he still had his .45 and ample ammunition, but right then no target. *Come on, Charbonneau, show yourself. I don't have all damn day.*

Bodie couldn't rid himself of the image of Sam Trask, safe at the moment inside the house — but, he reminded himself, with two innocent people close by. He refused to discount the fact that Trask was a wanted man, on the run and close to getting himself taken in. They had already come close to a confrontation just about the time Charbonneau and his partners had shown up. Trask had used the coach crash to effect his earlier escape. He might do the same while Bodie was distracted by having to face the three mustangers. For all the manhunter knew, Trask might already have slipped away from the house and was on his run for the Canadian border. He had no proof; all he had was guesswork. Yet it crossed Bodie's mind that it was what he would have done in the same situation. Trask wanted his freedom. He wasn't going to sit idly by while an opportunity presented itself.

It was time to make things happen. Bodie made sure the rifle was primed and ready. He gripped it in both hands, took a breath and broke away from his position, making a rush for the other side of the stable opening. He almost forgot Royster was sprawled across the doorway, and had to make a hard step over the body.

The crash of a shot came just as he reached the other door and felt the slug pluck at his sleeve. He reached cover and told himself it had been a damn fool move, but he had needed to get Charbonneau to open up. Foolish or not, he had a result — apart from a tear in his shirt sleeve — because he had picked up the brief flash as Charbonneau had fired. As he pressed against the stable side, he pinpointed the spot.

Another shot put a slug into the door. Bodie caught the gun flash. It came from behind a large stack of cut wood. Focusing on the place, he made out a part leg exposed at the corner of the stack. He brought the Winchester into position, finger curled against the trigger. The sheeting rain made it hard to see the target clearly. Bodie knew he wasn't going to get a better shot. He settled his aim, fired, and saw the leg jerk aside as the .44–40 slug shattered Charbonneau's knee in a burst of red. Bodie levered a fresh shell into the rifle's breech, stepped out from cover, and crossed the yard at a loping run.

Above the rain, he heard Charbonneau's pained cursing. He saw the man stumble into view, slumping against the wood pile, but still trying to bring his own rifle into action.

'Leave it!' Bodie yelled.

' . . . crippled me . . . ' Charbonneau said fiercely. His rifle rose in an unsteady arc. He was hurt but still made his attempt.

Bodie fired from the hip, a continuous burst of fast shots that ripped into Charbonneau and turned him half around. He pitched face down in the mud, arms thrown wide, and didn't move again.

Bodie stepped out of the stable and walked towards the house. He was concerned now about Gibbs and his daughter. The gunfire could have alerted Trask.

He was only feet away when he heard shots coming from inside. He jacked a shell into the Winchester, hit the door with his foot, and sent it crashing open. He took in the scene that confronted him, and even his senses were jarred.

Jessie Gibbs and her father were on the floor, blood already spreading from beneath them. Isaac Gibbs had a mangled head wound, the back of his skull shattered. Jessie, face down, had bloody wounds in her back. Standing close behind was Sam Trask, the pistol in his hand still smoking.

The moment Bodie was framed in the door, Trask turned his raised pistol and fired. Bodie felt the slug thump against his chest, pushing him back-wards. A heel caught in the bottom edge of the doorframe and he went down on his back, feeling the chill of the rain hammering against his face.

He thought it was a damn silly thing to do just lying there ... but the strength had already started to fade and his will to get up went with it. He made one last effort before his body closed down and the day went black ... blacker than he had ever known before ...

12

'I had a feeling you would be back, Herr Bodie.'

The voice came from a long way off, or so it seemed to Bodie. He was slowly rising out of the darkness that had enveloped him when Trask's shot had hit him in the chest. Right now he was so far away from reality that nothing really made any sense. The shot had been the last thing he could clearly recall. Being hit. Falling. Cold rain on his face. Nothing after that until he . . .

He knew the voice. Doc Meerschaum.

Meerschaum's broad face swam into focus. He nudged his spectacles into place, frowning as he peered down at Bodie. He shook his gray-haired head, but failed to hide the hint of a smile on his face.

The irascible medic who had treated

him earlier. If that was true, then was Bodie back in Colton? And how had he got there? Certainly not under his own steam. Not with a slug in him . . . He felt the dull ache then in his upper chest. A deep pain that grew as he concentrated on it.

'Damn it hurts.'

'Of course. You have been shot. I took out the bullet, but it was tight in your chest muscle and I had to fight to get it out.'

'Hell, Doc, what did you use? A bent spoon?'

'You are *glücklich*. A lucky man, Herr Bodie. Those thick bindings I wrapped around you for the ribs, they acted as a barrier and slowed down the bullet. Your muscle did the rest. They stopped the bullet from going in too deeply. As I said, *glücklich*.'

'I don't feel too lucky, Doc. Not right now.'

'You complain. Now I know you will get better, manhunter.'

Bodie swallowed with difficulty. His

mouth was parched. Meerschaum noticed his discomfort and produced a cup of water. He raised Bodie's head and got him to drink. The effort left Bodie feeling weaker than he had for a long time, and it was a relief when Meerschaum lowered his head back onto the pillow.

'Last I recall, I was way up in the hills. How'd I get back here?' he asked.

'A couple of trappers happened by. According to what they told me, it was like a massacre. Three dead outside. Two more shot inside the house, and you.' The voice was Ezra Pointer's. The marshal stepped into view at Bodie's side. 'You want to fill in the blank spaces for me?'

'I trailed Sam Trask to the Gibbs' place. Didn't know he was still there until I went inside to get out of the storm. He was calling himself Kincaid. I recognized him from the wanted poster. Didn't let on I knew who he was in case he threatened Gibbs and his daughter. I let him believe I was a passing stranger. Went out to the stable to check my horse, figuring to move in by the back door and get the drop on him. Only I hadn't counted on three of Cabot's mustangers riding in. They cut loose and we went at it. I walked away. They didn't. I went back to the house, heard shots and went inside. The Gibbses were already on the floor, and Trask cut loose the minute I stepped up to the door . . . I walked into it like a damn tenderfoot.'

Bodie felt weary after his speech. Even talking was hard work at the moment.

'Fellers who hauled you back here said Gibbs and his daughter had been shot in the back. They were both dead. So are the three mustangers. Trappers found fresh horse tracks leading away north from the spread. Looks like Trask took a couple of horses.'

'He's picking up his trail again,' Bodie said. 'Going for the border.'

'Leaving dead people behind him,' Pointer said. 'I have a feeling he's going to get away this time.'

Bodie stayed silent for a while, working on the fragments of memory that were floating around inside his head.

'Marshal — Ezra — I have an notion I want to share with you.'

'You wish me to leave you alone with the marshal?' Meerschaum said.

'No. I need sensible heads on this, because I don't want you thinking I'm talking like a crazy man.'

'Go ahead,' Pointer said.

'Linus Dorn.'

'What's he got to do with anything?'

'Bushwhacked me before I found the Gibbs' place,' Bodie said. 'Only he didn't make it.'

'Dorn? Why would he try to kill you?'

'So you knew him?'

'He was known around Colton,' Pointer said. 'Mostly in the saloons. No good way to tell it but the truth. He was a drunk. A barfly. Spent his time begging for enough cash for his next bottle. Took any job he could to earn a few dollars. You're telling me he tried to shoot you?'

'Yeah. He took money to follow me and take me down.'

'He tell you who paid him to do this?' Meerschaum said.

'Lucinda Montefiore,' Bodie said without hesitation.

'As in Monty's Restaurant?' Pointer said.

'The same.'

Pointer looked across at Meerschaum. The doctor returned his gaze and the pair of them stood considering what Bodie had just said.

'You know, Bodie, since you came to Colton, things have been happening,' Pointer said, 'but this is the strangest.'

'I ain't making it up. As soon as I mentioned I was after Trask at the mustangers' camp, they jumped me. Tessler pushes me into a gunfight. Now that restaurant woman hires someone to shoot me. I'll agree there's something odd going on. I just wish I could figure out the connection to it all.'

'Maybe the connection is Cabot and this Monty woman,' Meerschaum said.

Bodie rolled his head on the pillow and stared at the doctor. 'What makes you say that?'

'Cabot and the woman, they are — what you would say? More in command. All the others follow. Cabot's hired help. This man Dorn. Am I right?'

'If we accept that,' Pointer said, 'what is Sam Trask to them?'

'Maybe family,' Bodie said. 'There has to be a close tie for them to do the things they have.' He turned to Meerschaum. 'Doc, was it dark when I was brought in?'

'Ja.'

'Those fellers who helped me — they still around?'

The doctor shook his head. 'When they left you with me, we talked and they agreed they would ride back to the Gibbs' place to bury the dead.'

'They came to see me,' Pointer added. 'Said it was the Christian thing to do. I know those men. They'll do the right thing. Why'd you want to know?'

'If that's so and they rode out, likely the Monty woman doesn't know I'm back in town.'

'What you planning, Bodie?'

'First a good night's sleep. Come tomorrow, it might be we can help things along.'

13

Will Cabot came into town quietly, easing his horse along the back lots until he reached the rear of Monty's Restaurant. It was full dark, late, the way in shadow as he eased out of the saddle and stepped up to the kitchen door that stood partway open. A light still showed inside. Monty would be cashing up, the staff gone for the night. She did this every night after the close of business. Cabot paused on the top step, looking into the kitchen, and saw her at the kitchen table, bending over the paperwork.

'Never adds up the way you expect,' he said.

The woman glanced up, lamplight creating shadow across one side of her face as she moved. Any surprise she might have had vanished quickly.

'You can say that about life in

general. Now what are you doing here? Did anyone see you?'

'I came in from the far side of town. Never showed myself on the street.'

Monty pushed aside her paperwork and stood. She crossed to the big cooking stove, where a pot of coffee gently steamed. She poured into a pair of china mugs from the side, handing him one.

'I ran into three trappers on the trail. They'd called in by the Gibbs' place. They found Charbonneau, Royster and Kellin. All dead. Looked like a set-to. I sent them to deal with that Bodie feller, only it hadn't worked out. They found Gibbs and his daughter backshot in the house. There was also Bodie, shot as well. And there were tracks heading away from the place. Single rider leading a spare horse, heading north.'

'Will, I sent Linus Dorn out to — '

'That barfly? Christ, Monty, that was a damn stupid thing to do.'

'Your three boys don't seem to have done any better.'

114

'Yeah, well, it's done now.'

'If Bodie hadn't shown up in Colton, none of this might have happened. Well at least he's out of the way now.'

Cabot shook his head. 'But he ain't. He's still alive. Those trappers brought him to town and left him with Meerschaum. I met up with 'em on their way back to the Gibbs' place. They were going to bury the dead.'

'Bodie's here in town? If he tangled with Linus Dorn, maybe he knows I sent him. Damn, Will, what do we do now?'

'it's tolerable late to be asking me that now.'

Monty stared at him, anger in her eyes. 'Will, I don't know how to deal with this on my own.'

'Then we admit we're in a mess. And Sam is running wild, out of control. All the killing, the thieving . . . It's our damn fault. We should have done something years ago.'

'Done what?' Monty slammed her coffee mug down on the table, spilling the hot liquid. 'Had him locked away in a lunatic asylum?'

'Thinking back, that's just what we should have done. He's sick, Monty. Sicker than we've ever admitted. Goddamn it, we've always known that. We were wrong to leave him free.'

'Will, he's our son!' Monty screamed, losing control. 'Our son!'

'I've let you use that over the years. Allowed you to cover for him. Done it myself to back you. Monty, we're as responsible as he is.'

'No. He doesn't even understand himself what he does is wrong. He just . . . goes a little wild sometimes.'

'Wild? Dammit, Monty, he goes more than just wild. Look what he's done! What we've pretended hasn't happened! It has to end, here. I won't allow Sam to cause any more misery the way he already has.'

'No, Will.' She caught the expression on his face. 'What are you going to do?'

'Tell Ezra Pointer the truth. That we know all about Sam. What he's done.

It's time to put things right, like we should have done years ago.'

Monty stared at him, realization dawning on her as his words sank in. A cry of anguish rose in her throat. She let out a shrill wail and stared around her, lost, seeking some kind of comfort. When she failed, she reached for one of the cook knives in the drainage board beside the sink. Cabot saw what she was doing and moved to stop her. Yet she moved faster than he anticipated and lashed out with the heavy blade.

'Damn you, Will, I won't let you help them take my son. I can't . . . not my boy . . . '

Her first lunge caught Cabot across his left hand, the keen edge of the knife slicing a deep, raw gash in his palm. Blood surged from the wound and Cabot drew back, a hiss of pain bursting from his lips. As he pulled back his hand, blood flew in a bright spray.

'Jesus, Monty, not this way . . . '

Cabot's plea was lost on the woman.

It was as if he was talking to a shadow as she lunged again, reason lost in the sheer panic brought on by the chance of losing her son forever. Her onslaught was all the more frightening when he saw the bright unreasoning gleam in her eyes, the lips peeled back from her teeth in a grimace devoid of any feeling. His concentration lost for the moment, Cabot failed to avoid the increasingly wild slashes from the knife in her hand. He felt the cold slice as it caught his cheek, laying open a deep cut that sent blood streaming down his face.

Now she was screaming in an unending flow. Cabot took more cuts to his hands as he raised them in defense, and when he tried to grasp her knife hand she slashed at his arms, cutting through his shirt with frenzied strength. Cabot fell back, dislodging pots and pans from the work space behind him. Above the clatter of iron implements, he could hear Monty's cries of rage, a sound that cut through him as deeply as the knife cut through his flesh.

Cabot stumbled, as much from the wounds as from the shock of her raging attack. On his knees, despite his physical strength, he felt helpless under the rage of Monty's onslaught. It was primal and unstoppable, the instinct of a mother desperate to defend her child, no matter how badly he had acted. No matter the terrible things he had done.

The bloodied knife descended, cutting a deep gash across the exposed back of his neck, and Cabot had no more strength to resist. He slumped forward, oblivious now to the pain, to the blood pouring from the mass of wounds, and offered no more resistance as the knife rose and fell again and again, accompanied by the shrieking cries of the woman . . .

14

When Ezra Pointer had come to Bodie's room to tell him what had happened, the manhunter had insisted on joining him at the restaurant. By the time Bodie made his slow way across the street, a crowd had gathered outside. Even though it was still dark enough, people had been alerted by the screams coming from Monty's Restaurant. What they found had been enough to make them step back and stare.

Pointer had taken charge, preventing anyone from going in once he had herded the onlookers out. When Bodie followed him inside and through to the kitchen, he found Meerschaum already doing what he could for Cabot. Bodie noticed the woman, Monty, sitting on a chair in the dining room, a blanket around her and being attended by

Pointer's wife. Monty sat as if in a trance. The hands clutching the blanket were streaked with blood, and some had splashed onto her pale face. Jen Pointer caught Bodie's eye, shaking her head slowly.

In the kitchen, Will Cabot lay in a wide pool of blood. He was also bleeding from numerous knife gashes to his arms, hands and face. When Bodie moved closer, Meerschaum glanced up. His sleeves were pushed back and his hands were red. He held Bodie's gaze for a few seconds before shaking his head.

'Too much,' he said in a quiet voice. 'It is too much.'

Cabot's eyes focused on Bodie. 'It came to this,' he said, forcing out the words through bloody lips. 'I should have let you go after him, Bodie. If I had, maybe Gibbs and his daughter would still be alive . . . now . . . I was trying to protect my boy . . . '

'Trask is the connection,' Pointer said. 'He's their son. Dammit, Bodie, they were trying to help him. For all the wrong reasons.'

'You should rest,' Meerschaum said, bending over Cabot..

'Doc, I'll have plenty of rest when I'm dead.'

'Why did this happen now?' Bodie asked.

'I rode in to tell Monty what happened over at the Gibbs' place. She just went crazy, scared she was going to lose Sam when I said I had to tell Ezra. But I had to do it. He's so out of control now, and good people have died. No more . . . no more . . . '

Bodie turned away and went back through to the restaurant. Pointer's wife left Monty and faced him. 'She hasn't said a word since we found her.'

'I'd guess she doesn't even know what happened herself.'

'When Ezra went in, he said she was just standing there with the knife in her hand, looking down at Will Cabot as if she had no idea what she had done. Mister Bodie, nothing like this has ever happened in Colton before.'

'I daresay you're right, ma'am.'

'It will take a long time to get over it.' Jen Pointer shook her head, lost for any more words until she said, 'What will you do, Mister Bodie?'

'What I was on my way to do when I came here. Find Sam Trask and bring him in.'

'Dead or alive?' Her words were cold, devoid of any emotion.

'Ma'am, that will be down to Trask.'

★ ★ ★

Will Cabot died before he could be moved from the restaurant.

Marshal Pointer locked Monty in one of his cells. He sent someone to the nearest telegraph point to summon a US Marshal. The killing was far beyond anything he felt he could handle, and Monty needed looking after by professional help.

After a restless few hours' sleep, Bodie organized himself. He topped up his supplies and made sure the chestnut was saddled and ready. He walked her down the street to the jail and tied the mare to the post, then stepped up on the boardwalk, feeling every move he made. The bullet wound was giving him some nagging pain, but he was damned if he would let himself be stopped by it. He pushed open the door and went in. Pointer glanced up from paperwork on his desk and indicated for Bodie to sit. The lawman poured coffee and handed Bodie a mug.

'Bodie, we're reaping the whirlwind here,' he said. 'I don't even have anyone I can send with you. No offense, but you're not exactly in the best of health right now.'

'You have a nice way of pointing out the obvious.'

'Trask has a hell of a start on you.'

'That too, but I don't have any other way of dealing with this.'

'He might believe you're dead.'

'I can't wait for the day I prove him wrong.'

'Bodie, how do people end up in such a bind?'

'Got me there.' Bodie downed a mouthful from his mug. 'I'm going to miss this coffee.'

'Jen brings me fresh refills all the time.' Then Pointer said, 'Monty talked to me a while back, only for few minutes. Clear as fresh dew. Then she went back to just staring at the wall . . . '

He explained that as Lucinda Trask, she had met Will Cabot when she was eighteen. They were two young people on a lonely mountain, and they fell for each other. She had a wild streak, and when he suggested they set up home together she agreed, because it was better than having nothing. They did so to the east of Colton, which was little more than a trading post back then. Will had his dream of becoming a mustanger and setting up his own outfit. He was young and full of dreams, and Lucinda wanted nothing more than to be with him and start a family.

At first it all worked out. Will built his horse ranch, drew in a crew, and they ranged across the Dakota Territory, seeking out the free-roaming wild herds. They caught their mustangs, corralled them and broke them in, selling to the plentiful markets. The demand for horseflesh was strong. Cabot's name grew; his reputation too. He drove his horses and sold them to the army and the distant spreads. And then Lucinda fell pregnant. She had a boy. They called him Sam, and for a time life was good.

The cracks began to appear before the boy was twenty years old. He proved to have a rebellious streak that grew and developed. Sam refused to take Cabot's name; he was Sam Trask. It was about that time when his errant behavior began to show. He fought everyone and everything and treated people badly, especially women. There were incidents — too many — and any attempt by Cabot to deal with them led to violent outbursts.

The younger man simply became too much for them to handle, and just after his twenty-second birthday a final confrontation erupted. After they fought, Sam rode out and vanished. It was the end of Lucinda and Will's relationship; it broke them up. She rode all the way to Colton and took a job waitressing in the new restaurant, where she soon became involved with Roman Montefiore. She married him and became known as Monty, working alongside him in the restaurant.

Sam began to make a name for himself — a bad name. He was linked with a number of crimes, though never caught, and he moved around, always one step ahead of the law.

Will Cabot threw himself into his business, roaming the Dakota hills and the surrounding territory with his crew and chasing the wild mustangs.

When Roman died suddenly, leaving Lucinda alone, she dedicated her life to the restaurant. Her relationship with Will took up again, but only as a bridge between herself and the estranged son, whom she saw on occasions when he snuck into town to see her. Will Cabot understood her need to see Sam. He covered for her, making sure she was able to maintain a discreet link. He carried a shadow of guilt that he had not done enough to help the younger Sam, and it was because of this that he made the effort to dissuade Bodie when the manhunter showed up at the mustangers' camp even though Sam was a wanted man, accused of rape and murder.

It all began to go wrong after that. Bodie did not back off. Tessler forced a gunfight and Bodie killed him. Monty's hiring of Linus Dorn failed, and when three of Cabot's men braced Bodie at the Gibbs' place they died. Sam lost all reason, and killed Gibbs and his daughter and even gunned down Bodie before he headed out for Canada. When Cabot told Monty he was about to confess to Ezra Pointer, Monty cracked and lashed out at him for what she saw as the betrayal of their son.

' . . . and that's how she told it. Doc believes she'll have a hard time coming to face what she did. May never.' Pointer stared down into his empty mug, shaking his head. 'Damned if I can understand half of this, Bodie. Give me a drunken cowboy on the weekend I'm fine. This is out of my reach, which is why I put out a call for a US Marshal. They got one coming over. We're lucky to have one in the area. The service is spread pretty thin out here. It's a big area and there are only a few men to go around right now.'

'He'll have enough to handle here,' Bodie said. 'All I need to do is find Sam Trask and finish what I started.'

'You make it sound easy.'

Bodie finished his coffee, stood, and held out his hand to Pointer. 'Ezra, I didn't say it was going to be easy.'

15

Bodie figured he had a good hour before fading light forced him to stop for the night. He had been moving north from the moment he had departed from Colton, through the day and now into the fading afternoon.

Before leaving town, he had spent time with Ezra Pointer going over the map of the area. Pointer knew the country and the trails that would lead to the border. He understood the formation of the hills; the high slopes and the likely ways a man on the move would take in order to clear his path to Canada. Bodie studied the big map pinned to the wall in Pointer's office and made his own mental notes, using a combination of the lawman's suggestions and his own skills as a hunter of men. He picked out the areas that would defeat a horse and rider;

memorized the open ways, the heavily timbered sections, and the spread of winding canyons that might lead a man to a dead end where he would have to turn around and go back. With the eye of a tracker well versed in following down a hunted man, Bodie saw the likeliest way Trask would go and followed his hunch.

Trask had not covered his trail during his first miles from the Gibbs' home. Then he had simply been running, making distance between himself and what he had done. Trask had acted hastily by killing the Gibbs, panicking because he had reacted to the gunfire outside the Gibbs' house, self-preservation dictating his actions. And when Bodie had made his appearance, Trask had fired on him without thought. Preservation had turned to panic, and Trask had run, stopping only to saddle his horse and take another for backup. He had ridden away from the refuge provided to escape, making his try for the

border and the vast Canadian landscape.

Bodie had picked up tracks from the
Gibbs' house: a ridden horse and a
second animal being led. Trask was
hedging his bets by taking along a
second mount. Being able to alternate
one for the other would give him an
advantage. He could ride for a time,
then change saddles to allow the first
horse to rest. Bodie realized he was
dealing with a man who had been on
the run before. Trask played a long
game.

The tracks, faint as they were, led
Bodie ever north and always climbing.
Trask was aiming for the high ground,
crossing the hills as he sought sanctuary
over the border. Bodie set the chestnut
on the trail, letting the animal find its
own pace as it began the long climb.
The chestnut was a powerful animal. It
had good staying power, and Bodie had
trusted it on many occasions. It had
never let him down.

When it got too dark to continue,

Bodie picked a spot and climbed down. He stood for a while, hand on the saddle, breathing slow and deep. He was stiff and sore. Doc Meerschaum had advised against making a long ride so soon and had voiced his feelings before Bodie had departed Colton. He had offered Bodie a bottle of laudanum to take if the pain became too much. Bodie had thanked him but declined. He understand the narcotic effect of the potion, and the last thing he needed was to be so sedated he fell asleep and dropped from the saddle.

'Doc, any discomfort I get will keep me awake. Last thing I need is to be riding around like a sleepwalker. Believe me, the only sleeping I'll be doing will be when I'm wrapped in my blankets on the ground.'

He had picked a spot near a stream that flowed down out of the hills, bordered by brush and trees. There was enough grass to keep the chestnut fed. Bodie let the horse drink, tethered it and off-saddled. He cleared a spot and built a small fire. Out of his possibles bag he produced what he needed: a small cast-iron frying pan and his battered coffee pot. He unwrapped a side of bacon and used his knife to cut a couple of thick slices. While the food cooked, he made himself a brew of black coffee. It might not have been the best meal he'd ever had, but at least it was hot. So was the coffee, and he managed three mugs before the pot ran out. From behind his saddle he loosened his thick shortcoat and pulled it on. He could feel the chill the night brought with it; and settling next to his fire, Bodie could hear the wind soughing down from the divide over to the north. The air had a distinct sharpness to it. He suspected that the temperature would drop even more, and he was grateful he had camped in amongst a stand of timber. It wouldn't stop the cold getting to him, but it would help.

With his blankets wrapped over his thick coat and his hat pulled low, Bodie leaned against his saddle and did his best not to feel too sorry for himself. He would have been the first to admit he was less than at his best. Since his arrival in the area, he had been pretty well battered about, then shot, so he figured he was allowed a little self-pity. He listened to the constant moan of the wind, hoping there was no snow around. That would just about be the last straw. Though it didn't offer him a deal of consolation, he realized Sam Trask would be having the same kind of uncomfortable night, unless he had found better cover.

Bodie had pulled his leather gloves on and tucked his arms around himself against the cold. For no discernible reason, an image of Ruby Keoh came into his mind — her cheerful face and long shining hair down to her shoulders. If she saw him now, she would most likely call him all kinds of a fool for letting himself get in such a situation, and in a way he couldn't deny the accusation. But this was what he did. It was his job, though it was risky and often downright dangerous. He put himself out on a limb chasing all kinds of wanted men, and for what? The rewards? Or the satisfaction of putting them behind bars?

It wasn't something Bodie gave much thought to. Maybe he should. Since meeting Ruby, there had been a shift in his life. That young woman had made a difference, he was unable to deny it; not that he actually fought against the notion. Ruby Keoh — young and beautiful, with a strong personality and a way with words that made him see the brighter side of life.

Right now, however, that was a long way from this cold dark spot on the side of a damn mountain somewhere in the Dakotas. If he hadn't been here, he could have been in some warm dining room in New York, sharing a meal with Ruby. A fine steak. A bottle of rich wine and a good cigar.

Close by, the chestnut snorted in

displeasure at the cold, stamping her hoofs.

'Yeah, I know just how you feel, horse. Just think yourself lucky. You carry your own fur coat around with you.'

He tugged his blankets tighter and let himself drift off into sleep. It wasn't easy, because Ruby's face kept appearing in his mind, smiling. Teasing. And always just out of reach.

* * *

First light brought a frost that covered everything. Bodie's blankets were stiff with the cold. Working his aching body into action, he coaxed his fire to life. His fingers were a shade less than numb, and he had to flex life back into them despite the leather gloves. He fed the fire, then got coffee brewing and bacon frying. He was definitely beginning to take a dislike to bacon at the moment. He found a couple of reasonably edible biscuits in his supplies and soaked them in the hot fat from the bacon. Downing the food and mugs of hot coffee helped to bring him fully round.

He pushed to his feet and moved around to bring some life into his stiff limbs, then washed his pan and coffee pot in the stream and packed them in the possibles bag. When he went through his saddlebags, he came across a bundle of thin cigars he'd forgotten about. He extracted one and lit it with a wood sliver from the dying cook fire. Bodie stood inhaling the smoke, and he could have sworn the tobacco eased some of his aches. He also knew he wasn't fooling himself, but it felt good for the moment.

As he pushed the other cigars into his shirt pocket, along with his wrapped supply of Lucifers, he felt he was being watched. It was the chestnut. She was eyeing him with a baleful stare. Bodie felt sure she curled her lips in annoyance.

'Fool horse,' he said. 'What good is a

damn cigar to you?' Using one of his blankets, he rubbed the chestnut's exposed back and flanks, removing the layer of frost. 'The things I have to do to keep you happy,' he grumbled.

The chestnut shook her head, making a soft nickering sound. While he dried the horse's back, Bodie checked the sky over the distant peaks. The morning light showed a moving bank of cloud that told him some bad weather was moving in. At this altitude, it could be rain — or even snow, the thought of which didn't make Bodie any happier. A fall of snow this high up would create problems for him. Travel would become difficult, and lowering temperatures would make life even more hazardous. Any tracks left behind could be quickly wiped away if a storm persisted for a long period. The only consolation was that the conditions would become difficult for Sam Trask as well as for himself.

He saddled the chestnut and fixed his gear behind the saddle, then led the horse to the stream and allowed her to drink. He refilled his canteen with fresh water and hung it from the saddle, then eased himself on board, gathering the reins and picking up the fading trail of two horses.

His line of travel took him from open slopes to timbered, across shale beds and hard pan. Bodie kept the chestnut moving slow and steady. The canny animal picked its way with care, negotiating the difficult sections with an almost dainty step.

As the day grew around him, Bodie was glad he had kept his coat on. The air against his face was taking on a decided chill. He had buttoned the coat up tight and favored the gloves he was wearing. A couple of hours in and the weather took a definite bad turn. The sky over the peaks became covered in heavy dark cloud. Hunched over, Bodie reminded himself of the dry southwest territory, where even the wind held warmth. Now all he could look forward to was more than likely freezing temperatures.

Moving along a winding narrow ravine with high slopes on either side, Bodie drew rein as he lost the tracks. He sat and cast around. Trask had come into the ravine and it was unlikely he had climbed out. The only way was forward. Bodie let the chestnut keep moving, peering at the hard ground. It took him almost a mile before he spotted disturbed stones, the darker undersides still showing where they had been overturned. He raised his eyes to check ahead and saw where tough grass stalks had been broken as horse's hoofs had passed by.

He noticed the light fading overhead as the threatening clouds closed in. Minutes later, he felt the first cold touch of snow on his face. The light fall persisted, gradually increasing until it gathered around him and settled.

Bodie settled in for the long ride ahead. He leaned forward and stroked the chestnut's powerful neck, using encouraging words. The horse would most likely be having similar feelings where the weather was concerned. He had no idea how long the snow might continue, or how heavily. The only thing he did know for certain was things were liable to get worse before they got better.

Late in the afternoon, Bodie came across the dead horse. It lay where it had fallen, the bones of its left foreleg showing through the flesh. He dismounted and checked the carcass. It had been dead at least a full day; maybe more, by its condition. There was a ragged bullet hole in its head.

An accident, most likely, maybe caused because Trask was pushing ahead without taking enough care over the uneven ground; and he had paid the price by losing his spare mount. Whatever the reason, the fugitive had forfeited some of his advantage. It would slow him some. Down to a single horse and with the weather closing in, Sam Trask wasn't getting his own way. He might find evading capture not such an easy matter.

The snow was falling heavily when Bodie decided to stop for the night. It had already dropped a good few inches on the uneven slopes, and the drift of wind buffeting down from the higher slopes did nothing to lessen the effect. With the ground underfoot thickly, layered, Bodie knew that combined with the oncoming darkness, keeping on the move was risky. So he looked for a place where he could make camp for the night. Shadows were lengthening as he came on a shallow ravine where part of one bank offered a reasonable refuge from the full drop of snow. It might not protect him completely, but he wasn't in a position to make too many demands.

'Looks like our spot,' Bodie said.

He guided the chestnut into a wide cleft in the side of the ravine. Snow had only drifted a few yards in and after that the broken rock was clear. It might change if the wind direction altered. Bodie saw it as his only choice.

He off-saddled and let the chestnut stand free. There was little chance the horse would wander. She had nowhere to go. The cleft petered out after a couple of hundred feet ahead, and the chestnut had the sense not to turn around and wander out into the snowstorm. Bodie laid his blanket roll on a smooth section of ground, settled with his back against his saddle, and lit up one of his cigars. He had no means of lighting a fire, so that meant no hot food for coffee.

'Whichever way you look at it, horse, we are damn fools putting ourselves through all this.'

The chestnut turned at the sound of his voice, lowering her head and fixed him with a look that seemed to agree with him.

Bodie hugged his coat tight around him, pushing his gloved hand under his arms. It was going to be a long, cold night.

16

US Marshal Alvin LeRoy rode into Colton with cold rain following him. It had already muddied the street. He reined in at the jail, dismounted and tied his horse, then stepped up to the door, opened it and eased inside. Heat met him, coming from the stove against one wall. As LeRoy closed the door behind him, Ezra Pointer looked up from the paperwork on his desk.

He took a look at the lean, strong-boned man. LeRoy was dressed in black, wide-brimmed hat low over his face. He gazed around the comfortable office with its polished furniture and saw a woman's touch. For a moment he was envious.

'Alvin LeRoy. US Marshal.'

Pointer watched him shrug out of the black slicker and hang it from one of the pegs next to the door. When he turned, the polished badge on his vest caught the lamplight.

'You made good time, Marshal,' Pointer said.

'The message you sent along suggested it was important.'

'That it is. Take a seat, Marshal. I daresay you could take a mug of hot coffee. Be with us in a while.'

As LeRoy dropped into one of the chairs, he took off his hat and brushed his hair back. Glancing around, he couldn't see any steaming pot on the stove. 'Am I missing something?' he asked.

'I own the store next door,' Pointer explained. 'My missus always keeps an eye out for visitors and brings in a fresh pot.'

'Nice arrangement. I'd say you have everything set out to your satisfaction.'

'We try to keep things civilized. Colton is a nice town.'

'Message I got tells me you've had some things happen of late that upset your peace.'

Pointer took out a sheaf of papers from the drawer of his desk and laid them in front of the marshal. 'I wrote it all out official-like, from start to finish. I expected that would be what you needed.'

LeRoy flicked through the documents. 'You've spent some time on this.'

'It warranted being done properly.'

'How about you tell me in your own words. I can go through the written report later. A man's words can make a difference in the telling.'

Pointer had barely said a few words when the office door opened and Jen Pointer appeared with her loaded tray. She placed it on the desk.

'Jen, this is US Marshal Alvin LeRoy. My wife, Jen.'

LeRoy stood and offered his hand. 'Ma'am.'

'You've made good time, Marshal.'

'Your husband's message reached me fairly close.'

'I hope this matter can be settled

soon. Nothing has ever happened quite like it before. Colton is generally a peaceful town.'

'Yes, ma'am. So your husband tells me.'

'I'll leave you to your business.' Jen Pointer lifted the checkered cloth covering the tray. 'Fresh coffee and some newly baked biscuits. Please help yourselves. A pleasure to have met you, Marshal LeRoy.'

After his wife had gone, Pointer poured coffee for them both, handing a mug to LeRoy. He settled with his own mug, gathered his thoughts and offered LeRoy the facts. 'It all really started the day the man called Bodie showed up in town . . . '

LeRoy was a good listener, only interrupting a couple of times to clear a point. By the time Pointer had finished, the marshal was on his second mug of coffee. He sat for a moment, seeming to be starting at a spot over Pointer's shoulder. 'You tell a good story,' he said. 'That all in your written report?'

'More or less word for word.'

'I wanted to hear what you had to say before I told you a few facts. I heard about Sam Trask from my friend Ed Pruitt. Trask is also known as Lester Kincaid and a couple of other names it might interest you to know. He has quite a reputation for cheating and trickery. Keeps on the move. He's a suspect in a number of murders. A bad hombre. It was pure luck he was caught and held recently. That's where Ed Pruitt became involved. He picked him up and was on the way to Yankton when their coach went off the road and Trask escaped. Pruitt was lucky to stay alive. The stage driver was shot dead. Pruitt called on Bodie and tasked him with going after the fugitive. I was going to head this way when I cleared up another matter. Then your call reached me, so I changed my route to Colton. What I didn't know was how bad things had gotten.'

'They turned really nasty when Will Cabot showed up in town. It all came out after the woman attacked Cabot. Nobody in town had any idea about the connection between Cabot and Monty, or that Trask was their son.'

'And she's locked up back yonder?'

Pointer nodded. 'Yeah. Doc Meerschaum has her sedated on laudanum. To be honest, after what she did to Will Cabot, we weren't sure how she was going to be. The doc said keeping her sedated was as much for her own safety as it was for anyone else's.'

'Damn, but this coffee is good. I may ask your wife to ride along with me and brew it up on the trail.'

LeRoy got up and looked at Monty, who lay on one of the cell cots, sleeping restlessly. 'Good-looking woman,' he said as he took his seat again.

'Always was polite and friendly. Ran that restaurant well enough. I can hardly believe the way it's turned out.'

'They do say the face folk show to the world can be just one side of the coin. Never can tell what goes on with the other.'

'So what happens now? How long do we keep her locked up here? The drunks I get from time to time usually sleep it off overnight and get booted out come morning. I can't do that with Monty.'

'She'll have to stay for the time being. I'll contact Yankton and see how they want to handle things. That's the best I can do right now.'

'I guess. This is going to stick with Colton and give us a reputation. Killings, murder, gunfight in the street . . . '

LeRoy nodded. 'And it isn't over yet.'

He was thinking about Sam Trask. The wanted fugitive. A killer on the run.

And with Bodie still on his trail, it most definitely was not over yet . . .

17

Sam Trask, also known as Lester Kincaid, Jack Bercow and Orrin Bassinger, was finding that multiple names were of little use, or comfort, when he was stranded on a rocky hillside in the northern Dakotas. He had ridden his spare horse over treacherous ground, causing the animal to step into a deep pothole and break a leg. He had ended the beast's agony with a single shot to the brain and had then allowed himself a moment of wild rage, cursing his foul luck, the world in general, and anything else he could bring to mind.

Only when he had screamed his way to silence did he sit down and allow his fevered brain to cool off. His wild rages came often, and when they did he was uncontrollable. Anyone around him during one of his spells could count themselves lucky to escape untouched. He was likely to lash out with his fists or anything he could get his hands on. Oddly, he only ever inflicted these murderous rages on women, never men. He had a particular obsession with hurting the female species. And as they were usually working girls, these indignities were regarded as hazards of the job and seldom reported.

Though it never came to anyone's attention, Trask's motivation for the violence was simple enough. He punished women to hit back at the mother he saw as having failed him; who had striven to better herself at any cost. That cost was near-abandoning him over long periods, leaving him with other women who were supposed to care of him while she was away. Unfortunately, most of those women were barely able to take care of themselves, let alone a young boy. And there were those who mistreated him. Over the empty years, that mistreatment came in the form of physical and sexual assault, leaving him bitter, full of hate towards the female sex, and yet still yearning for the love of a mother who only realized what had happened too late. The boy had been formed into a man who was near-incapable of true affection, and could only achieve his pleasure by hurting others, through violence or cruel sexual gratification.

He had made a big mistake when he had gone too far with one of his female victims. He had brutally raped her, and in his sexual frenzy he had beaten and then strangled her. One of the girl's friends had walked in before he could move on. She recognized him before he knocked her down and fled.

It wasn't the first time he had killed, but the only time it had been a woman. Trask understood the trouble he could be in if he was caught. Murdering a man was bad enough; the unwritten rules of the frontier frowned upon the wanton killing of women. He had marked himself by his actions and he knew he needed to clear out of the country until matters cooled down. If he could get across the border into the vast Canadian wilderness, he could lie low for as long as he needed.

Trask didn't concern himself too much with regret over the heinous crime. His unfeeling personality left him without the emotion. In his mind, the girl had been responsible for her own demise. She had fought him as he ravaged her, and that resistance had inflamed his rage. Once Trask was in that state of mind, reasoning vanished and there was nothing to hold him back. The only clear thing he could bring to mind was the fact that the girl's face as she died took on the look of his mother. It enraged him even more and forced him to intensify his act of brutality.

Knowing he needed to get away from the area, he had headed up country, taking himself by back trails and avoiding as much contact as he could. He only stopped to visit his father's mustang camp and talk his way into being supplied with a fresh horse and supplies. He made no mention of his escape from the law or that he had killed the girl and the stage driver. By the time the news reached the isolated camp, he would be far away, hopefully across the border and lost in the Canadian wilderness. He knew there was a poster out for him, bearing his likeness. It was as he was gradually working his way across country, avoiding communities, that he had called in at the place run by Isaac Gibbs. He had intended to take a couple of fresh horses before he rode further north.

The unexpected appearance of the man called Bodie, who Trask knew as a bounty hunter, had alerted him. It had only been the intrusion of the three men from his father's mustang crew that had given Trask the opportunity to turn matters to his advantage and escape. He had put Gibbs and his daughter down and had shot Bodie when the man stepped through the door.

Trask had used the time on his own to set himself up with a fresh horse from the Gibbs' stable. He had chosen a powerful dun-colored animal he knew could get him up country and across the border, as he was more than familiar with the way, having taken himself into Canada on a number of occasions when he needed to hide away and stay off regular trails. With his horse prepared and gathering supplies from the house, Trask had set off. He didn't hurry, because he felt safe in the knowledge no one knew where he was headed. He had dealt with witnesses, including the manhunter. And Bodie himself had put down the men his father had sent, so he was free and clear.

The inclement weather would help to hide his trail. Trask felt confident that his ride to Canada would be trouble-free. The country was big and thinly populated, and Trask knew places he could go to and stay.

Rain had given way to colder weather

that in turn brought snow down off the high peaks. It wasn't the first time he had faced the changeable climate here in the rugged slopes, so at first he was not overly concerned. He had buttoned up the long heavy coat he wore, pulled on thick gloves, and set himself for the ride ahead. The snowstorm developed into something he had not anticipated, however, and even Trask found himself foundering after a few hours. A look at the sky told him this was going to be a really bad storm. The temperature plummeted and he felt the cold despite his thick clothing. He felt the snow forming thin ice on his cheeks, clinging to his skin. The layer of snow on the ground slowed his horse as it plodded forward reluctantly. It hesitated a number of times and Trask struggled to keep it moving.

He realized he was going to need to find cover before too long. He could easily perish out here while this storm continued. Trask looked around. He was still able to recognize landmarks the storm had not yet covered. He turned the horse and crossed a stretch of ground that brought him to a rocky section where he knew there was a refuge, then eased out of the saddle, taking the reins and leading the horse the final yards that brought him to a dark space in the rock wall. It was the entrance to a cave Trask had used a couple of times previously. There was enough height to allow his horse to walk inside, and Trask led it in deep. A little drifting snow lay just inside. Trask knew the cave went back a long way into the rock formation and he would be protected.

He shook the snow off his coat and hat, then swept off as much as he could from the horse. In the light that came from the entrance, Trask checked out the space. He inspected the cave floor, noting that there were no signs of previous occupation, neither human or animal. He took his rifle and paced deeper into the cave formation. He knew it went back a couple of hundred feet, making a right-hand curve some way in. Partway along, water seepage had created a small pool where countless years had worn away at the rock to form a small pan. The water was always cold, summer or winter. As a priority, Trask went and collected his canteen, filling it with fresh water, then led the horse to the pan and allowed it to drink. From the substantial supply sack he took a bag of oats and fed the dun, then left it by the water, taking his possibles sack back with him, along with his blanket roll. He had taken food from the kitchen at the Gibbs'; cold meat and a loaf of bread. He had the makings for coffee but no means of having a fire inside the cave. He had found a half-bottle of whiskey at the house, so that was going to have to make do.

He placed his blankets on the floor as a cushion and sat with his back to the cave wall. From where he sat, he could see the entrance and the still falling snow. He ate, finding the cooked beef tasty. A swallow of liquor helped it go down. Later he rolled himself a smoke and watched the light fade outside. Shadows lengthened inside the cave.

Trask pulled his coat tight. He was not as warm as he would have liked, but at least he was out of the storm, and he was prepared to put up with a degree of discomfort. He could hear the dun's hoofs on the rock floor. It had been fed and it had water. It wouldn't be going anywhere. He stared at the open entrance of the cave for a while, and when he had finished his quirly he folded his arms over his chest and closed his eyes. He was asleep quickly as always.

Sam Trask never had problems getting to sleep. He figured it was because he had a clear conscience. He had never suffered guilt — not for anything he had done, or anything he thought. When he slept, with the snow swirling about the mouth of the cave, he slept with all the innocence of a newborn baby.

18

Light flurries of snow had drifted partway along the cleft but didn't reach where Bodie had made his bed for the night. He came awake with first light, climbing slowly to his feet and feeling every ache and sore spot.

Every time, he told himself, *you take a beating and still carry on.*

He knew it, and he did just the opposite of what amounted to good sense. If Ruby could see him now, she would not be amused, and he wouldn't blame her. He managed a grin at the thought.

Crossing to the chestnut, he laid the blanket in place, then swung the saddle across its back, causing a surge of pain from his ribs. Moving carefully, he cinched the saddle in place and loaded the rest of his gear, tying on his blanket roll and possibles sack. He hoisted himself on her back, took up the reins and guided the horse outside.

The night's heavy storm had abated for the most part; just a light fall still came down from the pale sky. At least the wind had dropped to a breeze. The cold air chilled Bodie's skin. He sat for a moment, checking the way ahead.

The fallen snow had laid a white blanket over everything, softening outlines and hanging from the drooping limbs of the trees. The low temperature had formed a light crust on the surface, the horse's hoofs making brittle sounds as it moved forward. Bodie patted the sleek neck, feeling the chestnut's flesh ripple.

'Let's find that sonofabitch,' he said. 'Maybe then we can both get some real rest.'

*   *   *

It was full light when Trask led his horse from the cave and mounted. Only a light snow was falling, the main storm

163

having spent itself out. He had given the dun the remaining oats and fed himself with the last of the beef, so at least any hunger pangs would be held off for a while.

He sat for a time, setting his trail. Despite the covering of snow that seemingly altered the lay of the land, Trask knew where he was. His gaze followed the higher peaks and was able to recognize particular formations. By his reckoning, he estimated another day would see him over the border. He took into account that his progress would be dictated by the snow covering the ground. It would slow him, and he would need to take extra care because any ground hazards were covered by the smooth layer of snow. He thought back to the accident that had lost him his second horse. He admitted that had been down to his own carelessness and taking risks. He had paid the price.

Trask kicked in his heels and the dun moved off, its gait cautious as it pushed through the snow. He didn't force the pace. The horse would find its own path. He kept his long coat closed tight around his body against the temperature, which was still low. Trask knew the higher he rode the colder it would turn. Before he reached the final pass through the peaks, it would get even colder. It was unavoidable. He could feel the chill starting to penetrate his clothing, and thrust his gloved right hand inside his coat. He wasn't about to risk having his fingers turn numb with cold, in case he need to get to his gun.

Sam Trask had found it wise to always anticipate problems. If something happened to present him with a challenge, being unable to react could turn out to be fatal. He hadn't stayed alive and free for so long because of making such mistakes. That was all it took — one mistake. Make that mistake, and it was the end.

Slow as his progress was, Trask figured he would at least reach the pass before dark. He might not ride through due to the weather conditions, which meant another night out here. He would be satisfied to get to the pass, and camping out on the American side was acceptable. There were difficult sections to cross taking the pass. Trask saw no reason to put himself in danger just to gain few hours. Slipping and falling into some deep crevasse was something he had no wish to face. He had already lost one horse due to his lack of care. He wouldn't let that happen a second time. A man would be foolish to chance such a thing. He had come this far and had no desire to give it all up now.

The dun labored along a long slope where wind had drifted the snow to a thin layer. In some sections Trask could see the fractured surface of the slope's surface. He let the horse rest and shifted in his saddle, turning his stiff body left and right to ease the muscles. He made no conscious effort to check behind him; but when he did look back the way he had come, a harsh sound came from his lips.

Far behind him, still on the lower slope but moving in a direct line that followed the tracks he had left since moving out from the cave, was a lone rider. He was too far away for Trask to recognize, but visible enough to see he was on Trask's trail.

There was no doubt. Trask was being followed. The rider came on, slow and deliberate, fixed on his path.

If he had been able to spot the rider, had Trask been seen as well? Something told him the answer would be yes.

Trask felt anger starting to bubble up from deep inside. He knew if he didn't clamp down on it, that anger would turn to blind rage and affect him so strongly he would not be able to control it. Right now, the last thing he could afford was to allow himself to lose that control.

He slid his rifle from the saddle boot and raised it. He had it to his shoulder before he saw the stupidity of his action. The rider was far beyond his rifle's effective range. The slug wouldn't even reach halfway before it dropped. But even if the rider had been within range, it would have been a difficult shot. Trask would have been the first to accept he was not that good with a rifle. At close range maybe, but not at a distance. He preferred the close work a pistol offered — or even closer with a knife. Really close when it came to employing the cold steel of a blade. Just the thought brought a smile to his face. Nothing suited him better than the feel of a silent blade slipping into yielding flesh and bringing the shocked expression to the face of the victim. Working a length of razor-sharp metal into a body, feeling it cut through flesh and organs, releasing the warm flood of blood . . . Trask was aware of the sensation of pleasure rising in his body at the images crowding his mind and had to push them aside before they took him over too much. If he lost track of what was important right now . . .

He jammed the rifle back into the

saddle boot and snapped back to reality. Clasping his hands across the saddle horn, he concentrated on the distant rider. He was still too far away to recognize. Not that it mattered in the end. Trask would blow him out of his saddle once he came into range.

Keep coming, friend, because I'll be waiting for you. The longer you take to get closer means the longer you stay alive.

But only until Trask decided otherwise. He liked the thought that this stranger, unwittingly riding directly into his sights, would only remain alive on a whim.

19

Bodie saw the distant rider pause. He felt certain Trask had seen him and was sizing him up. There was too much distance between them for the fugitive to do anything about it, however; the rifle Trask carried didn't have the range to reach him. Trask would think on that now and most likely consider waiting until his pursuer rode closer.

That presented Bodie with a problem. Trask was going to want to either kill him outright, or at least take down his horse and put him on foot. If that did happen, Bodie would find himself in a bad situation. He was going to need to stay well out of rifle range, yet still attempt to reach the man.

Bodie had figured Trask was aiming for the pass up ahead, which would take him over the peaks and into Canada.

From his observation of the surrounding formations in the area, the pass was the only viable way Trask could get through. His past knowledge of the territory would offer him this opportunity and Trask would take it. The thought of losing the man now, after all that had taken place, didn't sit right with Bodie. He never liked to lose. It was what defined him as a manhunter. His mantra was to start a chase and not quit until it was settled. It had been that way from day one, and Bodie had no intention of going back on it.

That went double where Sam Trask was concerned. His actions had put him at the top of Bodie's current list. Too many people had died or been hurt. All that was down to Trask. Wrongs that needed redressing. This pursuit had a personal edge to it now. The Gibbs apart, Bodie had his own score to settle. Trask had shot him out of hand, and Bodie knew he had been lucky the slug had not caused him more damage than it had. It had been bad enough: the wound still made itself known as a persistent ache that acted up each time he put pressure on it by arm movement. That was something Bodie was living with. It was near impossible to make any move without it affecting the sore muscles. If life had been just, Bodie would have been taking it easy in some warm place where the only exercise his arm received was from him lifting a glass of whiskey. That was something he wouldn't be doing for some time yet. Instead he was riding up a snowbound mountain slope, close to freezing off his butt as he sat a rocking saddle. Somewhere in there, he figured, things were far from perfect.

'We doing the right thing, hoss?' he said. 'If I was being honest, I'd rather be enjoying some California sun.' The chestnut shook her mane, nickering in agreement.

He stretched his body, standing in the stirrups to ease the ache in his legs. All the while he kept the distant rider in his sights. It would be easy enough to lose him. The last thing Bodie wanted was for Trask to vanish. If he did slip from sight, it would be an easy matter for him to pull down into some hollow or behind a suitable boulder. Hiding from sight would allow Trask the chance to wait for Bodie to ride closer while he kept him in his sights, ready to take the shot that would empty the chestnut's saddle, and . . .

'Damn, I'm getting morbid.' Bodie raised his face to the sky and allowed the chill of still falling snow to enliven his skin. When he lowered his gaze, he saw that the distant rider was on the move again, still heading for the pass. He giggled the chestnut forward, determined to maintain his own line of travel, and not to let Trask slip away and lay in wait for him.

Bodie pushed the chestnut to a faster pace, wanting to close the gap a degree. He had little choice in the matter. If he allowed Trask too much grace, the man might breach the pass way ahead of him, and that would give him the advantage. Knowing the man, that would work in Trask's favor.

They traveled in this fashion for the next few hours, neither of them giving anything away to the other, both seeking the opportunity that would gain them an edge over the other. The morning slipped away, then noon; and in the early afternoon the snowfall increased again, sending wind-driven flurries across the slopes from a sky that threatened even more.

20

Trask found the way ahead growing steeper. He could feel the dun struggling as it combatted the incline and the deep layer of snow covering it. A couple of times he felt the horse miss its footing and slip back on its haunches as it pushed to regain its balance. He could feel its muscles tense, and heard the snort of anxiety as it strained against the pull of gravity. He eased out of the saddle, gripping the reins as he moved ahead, pulling and coaxing the animal. Snow knicked up from beneath the dun as it fought to stay upright. He saw its eye roll as a moment of panic seized it. Trask pushed back his own fear, not wanting the horse to feel his mood, and he spoke to it in a calm tone, aware that any untoward show of displeasure would only serve to scare the dun. He dug in his heels and kept up the pressure on the reins as he reassured it with his own voice. It felt like an eternity before man and horse reached a flatter section and the scare passed. Trask stepped close, stroking the nervous animal, using a gentle tone of voice to soothe it.

Under his thick coat, Trask was sweating from the effort. He calmed his breathing and leaned against the dun, peering across the saddle. Back down the long slope and even through the swirl of eddying snow, he could see the rider. Still coming. Still on his trail.

Trask felt the hot anger threatening to rise again. Damn the man, would he never quit? He knew the answer even as the question formed in his mind. Whoever the rider was, he maintained a dogged pace.

As Trask watched, a suspicion began to form in his imagination. He was sure it was nothing more than that. Simply a creation of his overworked mind. Because Trask was almost ready to believe the man following him was Bodie.

That couldn't be. He had shot Bodie, face on, back at the Gibbs' place. Had seen him go down with a .45 slug in his chest. The manhunter had to be dead.

He had to be. It had been a killing shot, he was sure of that. Even if Bodie had only been wounded, that kind of hit would have kept him on his back for a long time.

Right?

The man would not have been able to fork a saddle and ride all the way up the mountain slopes. Bodie was tough. A hard man. But even he couldn't . . .

Yet the longer he studied the oncoming rider, the stronger his conviction became. If anyone could do it, Bodie was the man. His persistence, often under difficult circumstances, was why his legend had grown. Was why he was called the Stalker, the man known to follow a trail as far as it went. The manhunter who never backed down. Who, it was said, would crawl on hands and knees to reach his quarry.

Bodie would follow a man to the front door of hell and challenge the Devil himself to give up his man.

It had been a long time since Sam Trask had experienced a moment of fear. He was doing it right now. For long seconds he allowed that fear to take over. He clung to his saddle and watched the distant rider coming on, getting closer with each second.

Bodie. Coming for him.

Just as swiftly, the lost moment was sucked away as the wind tossed around the falling snow. Trask slammed a hand down on his saddle, causing the dun to shiver.

No damn way. He wasn't about to let some bounty hunter snatch away his freedom. He was Sam Trask, not some piece of trash ready to be trampled over.

All right, Mister Bodie, you keep on coming, because I'm ready for you. The minute you're in range, I'll empty my gun in you and watch you bleed.

21

Bodie sleeved snow from his face, blinking his eyes to clear them. He stared through the drifting snow, picking out the still shapes of man and horse. Trask had been motionless for some time, and Bodie had the feeling the man was also studying him. He kept going, satisfied he was still beyond the range of the man's rifle. Beneath him the chestnut plodded forward, making no effort to move any faster than a walk. Bodie didn't push the pace. He had a feeling he was going to be spending another uncomfortable night on the mountain slopes, courtesy of Sam Trask, unless something drastic happened in the next few hours. The thought of that did little to improve his mood.

Above the drone of the wind, Bodie picked up another sound. He couldn't figure out what it was until the rumble increased in volume and out the corner of his eye he saw movement on the upper slopes.

An avalanche.

A huge body of snow breaking free from its situation and beginning the long tumble that would bring it down from the heights. It was a massive slide — tons of it moving in an ever-increasing flood, the sound of its passing becoming louder with each second, propelled by its own weight and gathering additional mass as it came on.

Bodie had seen avalanches before. They overwhelmed anything and everything in their path. The power was frightening. Nothing could stop them. They could sweep away people and buildings, the sheer immensity unstoppable. A cloud of finer powdered snow was created out of the bulk, misting the air like an icy fog. The speed of the avalanche grew as it rolled forward, spreading and intensifying.

And from its general direction, Bodie could see it was moving his way.

Sam Trask was forgotten. Pursuit of the fugitive vanished from Bodie's mind, because if he didn't get himself clear he could easily be caught up in the moving mass as it continued on down the slopes. If it reached and swamped him, he would end up buried beneath tons of suffocating snow.

Bodie jammed the Winchester back into the boot so he could grip the reins with both hands as he pulled the chestnut's head around and slammed in his heels. The powerful horse responded as if it realized the danger itself and thrust itself across the slope, muscles straining as Bodie urged it on with yells and shouts. Unmindful of possible hazards under the layered snow on the ground, Bodie guided the horse forward. The rumble of the avalanche grew louder, reaching a crescendo as it boiled across the lower slope.

The chestnut reacted to Bodie's frantic urging, sensing the danger that was bearing down on them. It gave a shrill sound, muscles tensing as it plunged through the layered snow covering the ground.

In a moment of clarity, Bodie spotted the lip of a gulley in front of them. He had no idea how deep it might be, or the steepness of the sides. He only knew it could offer a refuge from the onrushing flood of the avalanche. He couldn't hope to outrun it, or battle against it. So he rammed in his heels, yelling wildly at his horse to keep moving.

The chestnut, at full stretch, took the lip of the gulley, all four hoofs leaving the ground as it cleared the rim. In the moments before they dropped, Bodie felt the icy breath of the avalanche as it overtook them. That was all he recalled. The world vanished in an enveloping fog of white, dense and having enough force to take him and the chestnut down the gully slope. Bodie did his best to stay upright and failed. He was swept from the saddle.

He felt himself turned in every direction, not even aware which way up he was. Soft snow was all around him, lifting him, dropping him and pushing the breath from his body. It felt as if he was being crushed. Snow blinded his eyes, filling his mouth and chilling him to the point of freezing. His hearing was overtaken by the raging sound of the avalanche; and even though he was yelling, he was unable to hear his own voice. Time didn't mean a thing any more. He had no way of knowing how long it went on . . .

. . . until he realized he was no longer falling, tumbling, and the roar of the avalanche had ceased. He was surrounded by silence. Total and absolute. He lay still because he had no way of knowing which way he was lying; wary in case he was injured and any movement might cause him pain. Bodie flexed his fingers in the thick gloves. They seemed fine; cold but not damaged. He moved his booted feet. Again there didn't appear to be untoward injury. He moved his head, eyes catching light above him.

Daylight?

If that was the case, at least he was lying face up. He moved his right arm, pushing it through the surprisingly soft snow, and his hand broke free, allowing more light to show. He pushed and wormed his body up, moments later arching clear of the snow covering him. Bodie sat upright and took a look round.

The gully had filled with snow, almost to the level of its banks, but his luck had held. He turned his head and stared up at the high peaks. They all looked calm and settled again after dropping tons of snow down on the lower slopes. The gusting wind caught eddies of the still falling flakes and created misty swirls, but the avalanche had worn itself out. It was the way with them. They came out of nowhere, made their presence known, then ceased.

Bodie pushed to his feet, feeling the discomfort of his bruised ribs and the bullet wound. The way he had been thrown about during the snowfall had done him no favors. He ached fiercely — but at least he was still alive. Shaking off clinging snow, he brushed his right hand across his side and found the Colt still in its holster. He drew the weapon and shook snow from it, working the action and spinning the cylinder. He recalled having pushed the Winchester back into the saddle-boot, so that would be . . .

He thought about the chestnut then. His horse. As if it had read his thoughts, he heard its aggrieved protest coming from close by. Bodie followed the sound and saw, yards away, the bulk of the animal as it pushed its own way out of the layer of snow. He crossed to it, grabbing the reins, and encouraged the chestnut to work its way upright. The horse, plainly disgruntled, made a big fuss, kicking snow in all directions until Bodie talked it down. On its feet it skittered back and forth, snorting guests of air from its nostrils and generally playing up. Bodie let it have its moment, talking to it and stroking its heaving sides. When it finally calmed down, Bodie inspected it for any injuries. Apart from having lost its dignity, the chestnut was unhurt.

'Our lucky day,' Bodie said. 'If you can call it that.'

He took the reins and led the chestnut up the rise to the trail they had been walking before the fall of snow. It lay under a deeper layer of snow now, but from its general shape Bodie recognised it. It took a while before he pulled the horse through the tumbled piles of snow and stood with the defined outline of the pass ahead of him again.

He reached and slid the Winchester free. Checked it over. It hadn't suffered any apparent damage. The feel of the rifle in his hand reminded Bodie why he was here. Sam Trask: Bodie's sole reason for being stuck partway up a mountain in freezing weather. The fugitive was leading the manhunter on a trek that was fast building up to becoming the reason one of them was going to end up dead.

Trask wasn't about to give himself up, and Bodie had no intention of backing off. Somewhere between there had to be a reckoning. Bodie was damned if he was going to be the one who failed to walk away.

That might have been decided already, however. Trask had been caught in the avalanche too, and for all Bodie knew, the man might not have survived. There was a chance he might be buried under tons of snow. It was a possibility.

Sam Trask dead. After the long pursuit, the mountain might have taken him out of Bodie's hands.

Bodie didn't believe it for a minute.

22

Trask couldn't believe one man could have such bad luck. When he had dragged himself from the snow and stood gazing around, clasping a hand to his head where a deep gash was streaming blood, the first thing he saw was his horse. The dun lay yards away. Still. No sound or movement. He stumbled his way through the snow to stand over the horse and bent close to check.

It was dead. When he walked around it, he saw the gaping wound that exposed its side, the bloody rib bones crushed. Trask stared at the dead animal. The extent of the wound could only have been caused by a solid chunk of rock brought down by the avalanche, dislodged and impacting against the dun as it had been thrown by the snow.

Trask had lost a second horse. If he

had believed in fate, he might have figured he was being played; taunted by bad luck. True or not, he was still not having the best of times. He prodded the carcass with the toe of his boot, surprised at his own calmness. There was no raging anger; no swell of unreasoning fury that would have normally had him cursing in a fit of frustration.

The pain from his injury brought tears to his eyes. Sometime during the headlong fall in the aftermath of the sweeping avalanche, Trask had suffered a solid blow himself. The impact had left him dazed, his head battered, and he was sure he had passed out during the fall. Pulling a kerchief from his coat, Trask bound it around his head, wincing at the pain from the wound. There was little else he could do. Somewhere in the fall he had lost his hat and his rifle; the Winchester had been knocked from his hand during the time he had been thrown off his feet. He felt beneath his long coat. The pistol was still in his holster. At least he still had something to defend himself with.

That made him think about Bodie. He turned and searched for the manhunter, then picked up on the lone figure moving slowly up the slope, leading his horse. The man still had his mount.

Trask pulled open his coat and drew his pistol. He would take Bodie's horse and continue his way through the pass to Canada, and escape. He almost laughed. Maybe luck hadn't entirely abandoned him. He knew it wasn't going to be easy, however. Bodie was a tenacious son of a bitch. He would put up one hell of a fight.

All right, mister, let's see who can come out on top.

Trask checked the loads in his Colt, making sure all six cylinders held a bullet. There were additional loads in the loops of his gunbelt. He needed to get closer, within the range of the handgun. He had to make this count the first time.

He dropped to a crouch, lowering his bulk. From the way Bodie was moving, still leading the chestnut, Trask assumed he hadn't been seen. If that was the case, then maybe he would be able to close in on the man and get off his shots from close range.

The falling snow was lighter now but still offered some distraction as Trask edged his way forward. The main track he and Bodie had been following was at a higher level, so as long as Trask remained below it, his chance of remaining unobserved was better. His progress was slow. The snow underfoot was deep enough to hold him back, and Trask's impatience was threatening to get the better of him. He wanted the matter over and done with. He battled his reckless streak, holding down on his emotions. If he misjudged his timing, Bodie would react, and any element of surprise would be lost. The manhunter would not hesitate if it came to a split-second decision. His situation was as critical as Trask's. Any mistakes would cost one of them dearly.

A wave of nausea rolled over Trask. He dropped low, fighting the sickness. The pain in his head from the blow he had taken during his avalanche fall increased. Fighting back from expelling a groan, he touched the cloth he had tied around his head, and his gloved fingers came away sticky with fresh blood. He could feel it oozing down the side of his face. Not the time to find himself laid low. He needed to stay on his feet until he had dealt with Bodie.

Bodie's horse was his ticket to Canada. Freedom. His way of shrugging off everything that had gone wrong with his life. If he could cross the border, he had the chance to rebuild his life. Past associations would disappear. Trask could start afresh. He had money in the saddlebags still fastened to his dead horse; plenty to fund a good start.

And all that stood between him and that new start was Bodie, the damned bounty man who had dogged his tracks all the way from Colton.

The moment Trask recalled Colton, he experienced another surge of pain. That town and the association it represented — his parents; the two people who had let him down so many times. Their attempts to help had been too little too late. His pain pushed him to the ground, and Trask hunched over, waiting until it passed. He found himself wondering if the blow to his head was worse than he'd thought. Maybe he needed medical help. But that was out of the question while he was stranded on these mountain slopes, miles from any habitation, which made the need to get his hands on Bodie's horse even more important.

Pressed against the snowbank, feeling the chill touch of falling flakes on his face, Trask gathered his thoughts. Kill Bodie. Take his horse. Cross the border and ride to a settlement where he could get treatment. It all sounded so easy in his head.

trask forced himself to consider what he needed to do, and cleared his mind of all but his immediate thoughts. He glanced down as he became aware he was cocking and uncocking the Colt. The fingers of his gloved hand were streaked with blood from his head. He raised the hand to the improvised bandage and felt the wetness there. The wound was still bleeding. Not a good sign. He needed to move; to get into position so that when Bodie reached him, he would have the opportunity to hold him in his sights long enough for that killing shot.

But first he needed to rest, just for a couple of minutes until the nagging pain subsided. His vision might be affected by the pain, maybe even blurred. Coupled with the still falling snow, it was going to hinder him, preventing a clear shot. Trask couldn't allow that to happen. He might only get one chance at Bodie, and if he failed he would more than likely end up dead. Bodie's reputation preceded him. He had no worries about bringing in a fugitive dead.

Trask opened his eyes, startled into consciousness, and realized he had drifted. He twisted his body round and peered over the snowbank. A moment of panic seized him. Bodie was no longer in sight.

Where was . . . ? Then he saw the manhunter. He had already moved past Trask's hiding place. Trask realized he had missed the man as he drowsed. He could hardly believe his mistake, but held back from making any undue movement to avoid attracting unwelcome attention. Yet a bullet in the back would kill Bodie just as well as one to his front. There was still a way Trask could make this work for him. He had no worries about a backshot. In the end, what mattered was who was still standing when it was over. There was no one around to see whatever happened.

It was between himself and Bodie — and he had no conscience when it came to his own survival. He never had. It was too late to start now.

23

Bodie noticed there were no fresh tracks in the snow ahead of him. The falling snow was not heavy enough to have covered recent tracks so quickly. If Trask had passed by, his trail would still be visible.

Off to Bodie's side, a dark blurred shape caught his eye. He took a closer look and realized it was the bulk of a horse, part buried. He was able to make out the bloody wound in the animal's side. Trask's horse.

There was no sign of the man himself. The possibility of him being down there as well nudged its way into Bodie's mind. Maybe his earlier thoughts had been wrong, and Trask was lying under the snow, dead or injured. But there was no way he could go searching the area. Trask could have been thrown a distance and be down under feet of snow. The feeling he might never know didn't sit too well with Bodie. He liked to be sure that his quarry was dead. It was preferable to having a lingering doubt.

He stood in the silence of the mountain solitude, the snow dropping gently around him.

And it was that quiet that alerted him when his ears picked up a faint but unmistakable sound of a pistol being cocked. It was something Bodie was familiar with: the metallic click of a hammer going back as the weapon was readied for firing.

It came from behind him. Close. Too close to be comfortable.

Bodie didn't think too long. He let himself fall sideways, taking the impact of the landing on his left shoulder, dropping, twisting his aching body and ignoring the discomfort, because he knew if he didn't carry this off it wasn't going to end well for him.

The sound of the shot was loud. The encompassing silence of the high country seemed to amplify it. The shot missed, scorching the air over Bodie's moving form.

Snow kicked up beneath Bodie as he brought himself around, the Winchester snapping into position as he picked up on his target. Sam Trask, only yards away, a bloody bandage around his head, the glistening red running down the side of his unshaven face. His lips peeled back in a snarl of defiance as he made to adjust his aim. The long dark coat he wore flared open as he angled his body round, and the muzzle of the pistol gaped wide as it dropped in towards Bodie's prone form.

Bodie tripped the trigger and felt the rifle jerk in his hands as it let go its .44–40 slug. He saw Trask step back as the slug struck him in the chest. Bodie levered and fired again, then came up on one knee, still cocking and firing until the Winchester clicked empty.

He saw Trask fall back, his gunhand swinging wide. The pistol fired its final shot skywards. Trask hit the ground on his back. His front was bloody. So was the snow around him.

Easing to his feet, his abused body protesting, Bodie stepped forward and walked over to where Trask lay. The man still held his Colt. Bodie swung a booted foot and kicked it from his grip.

'If I'd gotten through the pass, I'd have had it made,' Trask managed.

'You'll never know,' Bodie said.

Trask stared up at the grim-faced manhunter. He made to speak, but nothing came from his mouth but a well of blood; and when his heart stopped beating, even that ceased.

Bodie leaned against the chestnut's bulk. His last reserve of strength drained away, and he felt he wanted to lie down and do nothing. What he had to do, however, was turn around and ride back down out of the high country, away from the snow and the cold, back to what passed for civilization in the Dakotas, and beyond. Well that would have to do for a start.

He took a final look at Sam Trask's

body, debating, then shook his head.

'The hell with it, horse. I ain't even going to think about hauling that all the way back to Colton. Anybody wants his body, they can come get it themselves.'

He jammed the rifle back in the sheath, then slowly, so slowly, hauled himself into the saddle and sat for some time until he had enough energy to tug on the reins and turn the chestnut around.

'At least it's all downhill going back,' he said. 'That's got to be worth something.'

Books by Neil Hunter
in the Linford Western Library:

INCIDENT AT BUTLER'S STATION

BODIE:
TRACKDOWN
BLOODY BOUNTY
HIGH HELL
THE KILLING TRAIL
HANGTOWN
THE DAY OF THE SAVAGE
DESERT RUN
ACROSS THE HIGH DIVIDE

BRAND:
GUN FOR HIRE
HARDCASE
LOBO
HIGH COUNTRY KILL
DAY OF THE GUN
BROTHERHOOD OF EVIL
LEGACY OF EVIL
DEVIL'S GOLD
THE KILLING DAYS
CREOLE CURSE